T0096780

JAPAN STORIES

In loving memory of May and Norman
and
Setsuko Taguchi

JAPAN STORIES

JAYNE JOSO

SEREN

Seren is the book imprint of
Poetry Wales Press Ltd
Suite 6, 4 Derwen Road, Bridgend,
Wales, CF31 1LH
www.serenbooks.com
Facebook: facebook.com/SerenBooks
Twitter: @SerenBooks

ISBNs
Paperback – 978-1-78172-589-4
Ebook – 978-1-78172-590-0

A CIP record for this title is available from the British Library.

The publisher acknowledges the financial assistance of the Welsh
Books Council.

Author photograph: Jayne Joso by Paul Musso
at the Hay Festival.

Printed in Bembo by Bell & Bain, Glasgow.

Contents

The artist must be blind to distinctions between 'recognized' or 'unrecognized' conventions of form, deaf to the transitory teaching and demands of his particular age. He must watch only the trend of the inner need, and hearken to its words alone. Then he will with safety employ means both sanctioned and forbidden by his contemporaries.

Wassily Kandinsky, Concerning the Spiritual in Art

Oona

I was worried about my heart. I don't know why. It's strange of me. I thought I should speak with someone. Maybe a mystic, my mother, a priest? Or keep it private? But then doctors? I would need them in the end. I chose a hospital. They couldn't find anything. Nothing wrong. Nothing, at all, was wrong. And so, I insisted. Check again, please. I was so very worried. What would I do if my heart were to fail completely? I knew it was broken. And I couldn't go on. I told them that. I told them. But the tests revealed nothing they said. Please! Run all of the tests just once more! Do it, check again! Sometimes, when you insist, something has to happen. Sometimes, something, will happen.

I have been fitted with a pacemaker. From now on it will do some of the work. My heart is assisted, it has help. And finally, finally, I am not alone. I do not have to rely only on flesh, only on blood. Not anymore. Part of me is mechanical and that makes me feel much better.

I needed that, inside my body. An electrical device and its tiny circuitry. They continued to say it. Nothing was wrong. Nothing at all. But I feel so much better. No longer am I frail. I am not just meat and bones and blood.

Namiko

Mr Yoneyama

It was usual, normal. Lovely and natural. All of these things. Mrs Yoneyama began to settle down on the futon with their three offspring, Chieko, Mieko and Taro. Three, five and seven. Girl, girl, boy. They had played late into the evening and finally it was time to turn in. They had kissed their father goodnight and little Chieko had run back for an extra squeeze, that spirit-lift of a hug. She had giggled and sighed. Then she ran off to the others and the calls from their mum to hurry now. School tomorrow.

Mr Yoneyama paused, feeling the tatami through his socks, placing his toes on the surface of the mat one by one, an easy exercise. A simple sensory pleasure. So necessary. He could hear his family's gentle chatter, laughs and cooing. His son argued a little with the eldest of his sisters, but his wife restored order so gently. It was her skill. The children.

He checked doors were locked, that things were in place, he dried a few things on the draining board at the sink. Switched out the lights.

They each called in turn *Oyasumi*, and he replied to their goodnight chorus with a shiver in his voice and somewhat quietly. It was usual, normal. What other families did. Sleeping, separately. Father. Family.

In the room across the way, mother and children were

choosing their positions on the large futon. They each shuffled about in their sleep, but so at ease with one another, so much at peace, a perfect murmuration.

My Yoneyama lay on his futon in a separate room. He had meant to tell his wife something. How he was feeling about work of late, how the pace of things was getting him down. How there was really quite some stress at the office. On his commute even, if he was totally truthful. And he had wanted to hear about her day, and wondered, was she happy? And yet they never really talked, there was never really the time, the space, the intimacy. But it's no good to wallow, he told himself. And he mustn't let himself get down. He should lighten his thoughts before sleeping. How to do this? He pulled his toes in under the covers. This season the nights held a chill.

He would like them to make a nice plan for the weekend. Yes, and certainly, about this, they should talk, they should talk a lot! A family trip. It could really be fun, bring them all together. But no matter just now. Tomorrow. Yes, he sighed, still the presence of stress in his heart. They could talk and plan tomorrow.

He listened to his family's gentle movements as they drifted further away and deeper into sleep. You cannot disturb such a scene, cannot add or remove anyone. The sleepers enjoy their skinship and it was essential. He knew that. It was good for the children, good for the mother. Good for each of them to be part of that.

He rolled over, his hand resting on the cold tatami. He had better try to sleep.

Sachiko and Saeko

Altogether things had worked out well. Sachiko, now newly housed, placed Panda on the cupboard by her books and moved Saeko san's kokeshi dolls to one side. That should be alright. Perhaps she could get a box and take them all upstairs and Saeko could find a home for them up there.

She pulled out the futon and lay down a moment to reflect on the day's events, for had she not been overheard in the local Seven Eleven, then for sure she wouldn't even be here. If her friend, Kaori, hadn't sounded so horrified that she was about to find herself homeless again, then Saeko wouldn't have taken notice, wouldn't have intervened.—Being nosy is one thing, and generally a bad thing, but taking a neighbourly interest in a young woman's plight is a sign of great empathy and care.—And so, a keen ear and the simple act of over-hearing had led to an offer by a kind stranger, Saeko, to take her in. For a fee of course. Rent. Sachiko wasn't a stray cat after all. Sachiko picked up on the dry wit, and though it would be easy to be taken aback, she rather liked it.

Saeko had shown the young woman around, asked if she minded living with small dogs as she had two, and offered her a modest room on the lower floor. A room she no longer used. It was dusty, but it was fine. It was small, very small, but it was fine. And it boasted its own neat bathroom, separate toilet and

21

a small kitchen area. Perfect just for one.

Saeko called down from the floor above. She was going to make them tea. There were things to discuss. Sachiko skipped up the wooden stairs and joined her new landlady, grateful and relieved to feel safe again.

There were a few ground rules for living in Saeko's house but nothing too heavy. And as they chatted away, soon on a lighter level, it was as though they already seemed comfortable with one another. Sachiko let her shoulders relax for the first time that day. The first time in a week! This was good, wasn't it? Really good.

Sachiko's eager optimism however, had run ahead too quickly and when Saeko began discussing her own life, she was quite the past master at appearing to be open whilst actually revealing very little. It made things somewhat uneasy. Saeko said that she was in her mid-forties, but to Sachiko she seemed older, perhaps by as much as ten years, more even. And she had a 'good job' and went out to work but it wasn't at all clear what she did. She danced around the topic, suddenly cutting to something more neutral. Tea. No, she didn't readily volunteer much real information about her world at all. – On their way from the convenience store earlier on, Sachiko remembered that the woman had told her that she wasn't married. *But had she been? Divorced then? Or had he died, and…? Gay?* Sachiko mused over questions that it wasn't polite to ask while Saeko fetched more tea, bancha and a plate of small sweet cookies from a local artisan store. They both knew the store well and this provided a very good, if overly formal moment between them, each recognising the other's good taste, and Sachiko was made to feel that she was being treated very well indeed being offered something she could ill afford herself.

Saeko knelt again at the other side of the table. Then, after sipping her tea and slipping off her socks, she produced a notebook and gently set out to address a list of necessary questions that she had written down, for, having taken in a stranger she had better make checks as far as she was able. It was clear now that the somewhat casual rules laid out earlier were just the opener and Sachiko now felt her character under scrutiny. But, as Saeko told her, there wasn't only herself to consider but the dogs. Two small Yorkshire Terriers now licked Saeko's toes and pranced about behind her picking up the cookie crumbs.

Sachiko endeavoured to answer as well and as honestly as she could. She was twenty-two, educated to high-school level, hadn't done very well, hadn't had a clear idea of her future, had favoured working in a bookstore, for example: an antiquarian one for that might be especially interesting. At this Saeko looked away and seemed to roll her eyes. Sachiko thought it best then to keep details to a minimum. In trying to sound interesting or something approximating a worthwhile human-being it might appear that she was showing off.

Is that true? About the bookshop? Saeko asked. Yes. It was. True. Completely. But somehow Sachiko found herself retracting what she'd said, for it did, just at that moment, seem untrue.

At present she worked as an assistant at a local kindergarten. Her role was to fill up the paint pots, prepare craft items, take the little ones to the loo and so forth. Saeko had stopped listening. She yawned. Then she stared at the backs of her hands. Did Sachiko enjoy that work? With children? Sachiko replied that indeed, she did. Both women fell quiet. The dogs sniffed about the tatami. Sachiko decided not to add anything further for fear, again, of appearing to embellish. Just the simple facts. Quick, short, clear. That might be best from here on in.

The rent was agreed upon, to be paid monthly, cash, in advance. No male callers, in fact, no callers at all without prior arrangement. But that all seemed fair and correct. It was quite a thing to let a stranger into your home, you wouldn't want them traipsing in a whole lot of other strangers too. And so, with all the uncomfortable money detail complete, it seemed that the dogs could finally be introduced. Rather strangely, it appeared that this was how the women would seal their contract, as though nothing more formal was required, no signatures, blood or sacrifice. The mood was once more friendly and easy. But just for a moment, Sachiko sensed that it was odd here, in this place, and with this woman. Really odd. She wasn't sure why. Just a sense of something. No matter. Silly to question things when they had just taken this wonderful turn for the better. For they had, mostly. And she liked dogs and permitted herself the easy distraction. Meet Mozart and Clementine! The names seemed to delight, and their owner heartily lapped up the flattery that ensued. Saeko, it turned out, had been quite the traveller in her youth. She had once tasted the sweetest clementine on a visit to Spain and had listened to Mozart in Vienna. She had danced a tango… somewhere; and in London, had tea at The Ritz…

The two little dogs were now permitted to cover the newcomer in kisses. They jumped on and off her lap in a frantic jealous game. Sachiko was not so much in awe as pleased by the stories behind the dogs' names and warmed by the inclusion in part of Saeko's private world. If all of that was real. If it was true. Probably it was. Mostly. People, some people, do live lives like that. For sure. Truly colourful lives. And anyway, what did it even matter? Everything would be alright, and living with sweet little pets would be so very lovely. Things were good. She petted the dogs and smiled.

Saeko pulled her *haori* about her, caressing her breasts a little as she did so and lowering her gaze. She wondered at how deep an impression she was having on the young woman whom she thought seemed almost to yelp in response to her stories of international travel and adventure. It was the same girlish sound used when she had witnessed her explaining her housing predicament to her friend in the convenience store. And it was nice to see this lack of control. It was fresh. Alive. It was the reason she had intervened so forcefully. Insisted she come and stay. She liked her. She liked the noises she made.

The dogs lay still now, licking their paws. Sachiko ventured back downstairs to her new home. The small bathroom would need a clean and she should bathe soon and sleep early ready for work next day. She ought to set about organising the small kitchen area too and when she had some spare cash, she would buy a few things, make it more homely. She flicked the old light switches off and on and felt a slight buzz of electricity. There was no running water in the small bathroom and the neat stove in the kitchen was disconnected. No matter, at least the toilet worked and for sure these other things were soon remedied. Loose connections, a tap that needs adjusting, probably not much more. She hesitated to climb the stairs again so soon and discuss the issues, so settled that she would manage with a quick freshen up in the bathroom at work the following morning, just this once, and Saeko would certainly have these things fixed right away. Besides, the conversation might become embarrassing and she didn't like to offend. She still had a rice ball in her bag from earlier and some chocolate. For tonight, that would suffice.

In the morning she left the house as quietly as she could leaving the landlady snoring in the distance and the two small dogs just the same.

At the kindergarten, Sachiko stole a little time to create some very special and intricate origami. Some extra fine paper had been donated to the little school and a few sheets wouldn't be noticed. When her shift was over, she placed the tiny paper sculptures in her bag and hurried to the street of artisan stores nearby and to Kaori's shop. Kaori had been her friend in Tokyo the last five years, the entire time she'd lived there. She had a tiny shop selling organic cotton dresses, each designed and made herself. The shop rent was so high that Kaori and her husband had moved into a tiny apartment in which they could barely move. It was piled high with Kaori's fabrics, her sewing machine, threads and paper patterns. It had often felt like a miracle that the shop ever came into being, but Sachiko had always encouraged her and cheered her on, and by now their friendship was deep. So much so that when previously made homeless, Kaori had made up a futon on the floor in her shop for Sachiko to sleep on. In an emergency this was fine, but it was impractical for more than a couple of nights and Sachiko always knew she had to find a solution fast. She took the special origami to the shop and threaded them together, hanging them about the shop window to Kaori's delight.

Kaori showed Sachiko her latest designs, heavy cotton dresses, knee-length with one wide pocket right across the front, nicknamed the kangaroo, and others with two large, deep pockets at the front – they joked about just how much you might fit in these, they were enormous. Kaori's colours this season were denim blue and chamomile, so lovely. Kaori told Sachiko to try one on as the shop was quiet. She did, and at the same time Sachiko ran through what had happened so far with Saeko at her new home. – It had been such a stroke of luck being overheard like that. – She told Kaori about Mozart and Clementine, and they agreed that a woman with such imagination and one who was also kind and well-travelled was surely a dream landlady. Sachiko also felt relieved that perhaps there wasn't much mystery about Saeko's life after all, she was eccentric, and an independent woman and both these attributes sat easily with her. They were things to admire, and the stories of adventure she realised were things Saeko would keep mostly to herself. She was honoured to have heard them. Not everyone gets such opportunities.

Still at the shop, Sachiko tried on a dress in the pale yellow with two large pockets. It felt so nice and Kaori said how cute she looked, but it was already time to hurry back to work. Origami and singing in the afternoon for the little ones. They hugged and Sachiko set off back to the kindergarten.

In the evening, Sachiko arrived back at the house to find the small stove connected and functioning. She smiled and put on some supper. Saeko called down to her. Would she pop up as soon as was convenient?

Sachiko went on up and gently called out, Saeko stood up and grimaced. What on earth was that smell? Was that what Sachiko took for cooking? She must not stink the house out like that. It was no way to reward her landlady after she had been to the trouble of fixing things for her. At some expense. And all her other kindness, to a stranger! – *was she drunk?*

The dogs immediately ran to Sachiko. She bent down to greet them and didn't respond to Saeko who now moved at speed to the entrance and helped herself to a slipper, hurling it at Clementine. You little bitch! You shit on Mummy's tatami! The little dog leapt out of the way and yelped as the slipper clipped her back end.

Sachiko also yelped. Saeko smiled inwardly at the reaction and her cheeks coloured, but she didn't look back at Sachiko. Sachiko had brought up one of her special origami sculptures to give to the woman, but now let it crush, softly, in her palm.

Saeko moved on now to the matter of the bathtub. Sachiko

should use the bathroom upstairs and take the bath water in the evening after Saeko had used it since Sachiko was younger. It did not make sense and was not environmentally conscious to run two bathrooms and heat all that extra water. Sachiko agreed, but was still flummoxed by the small scene that had just played out. The little dogs had become anxious and wary and now cowered, one in the small dog basket, the other under a chair.

Sachiko nodded agreement with all, whilst not being entirely sure what had been said or, what had just taken place. She feigned a smile and withdrew once more downstairs.

A bad day is all, Saeko was having a bad day, and at least she had fixed the stove and the bathing issue was now remedied. All would be well. Sachiko listened out to get a sense of when Saeko had finished with the bath, and then tiptoed up. It was dark save for outside street lighting that threw strips of light over the older woman's bare body. She lay prone on the tatami in the main room, the paper doors drawn back. Sachiko took a breath, but then she noticed the sleeping woman's chest move just ever so slightly. Her eyes were shut. But it was cold. No matter, she mustn't interfere or be thought to have been watching. As quietly as possible, she slid open the bathroom door and placed a foot inside. Saeko's voice broke the quiet. She wasn't asleep, she was merely resting after her hot bath and had drunk some whiskey, not anything Japanese but true whiskey she muttered, from Scotland. Steam escaped the bathroom, Sachiko nodded without any precise meaning and entered the bathing area, sliding the door to a close and using the tiny hook inside to keep it that way.

When she emerged from bathing, Saeko had withdrawn to her room, the little dogs were nowhere to be seen. It was quiet. Relieved, she returned to her downstairs den and laid out her futon and sighed heavily. She had a roof over her head, had eaten cooked food, and bathed. Good. It was all fine now. She would sleep well and be refreshed for the little children in the morning. They always cheered her up, but they took a lot of energy.

In the moonlight, she noticed the kokeshi dolls again, so she collected them up and stood them in a tall slender box. These dolls had always seemed creepy but most people loved them, she knew that; it wouldn't be easy to say she didn't like them, best just leave them downstairs, but at least in a box she wouldn't have to look at them. She lay Panda on her pillow. Night-time. Time to recover mind and body. Her head touched the pillow and she was out like a light.

Over the coming days, Sachiko tried to busy herself outside the house as much as possible, staying longer at work and helping out Kaori with the new stock and the layout of the shop. She felt that her moving in had somewhat unsettled Saeko, who had perhaps grown unaccustomed to sharing. She had been kind and generous in taking the risk of allowing a stranger in, and it was natural that it would take time for them to become used to one another, in a real sense. Smells, routines and habits. It wasn't personal, but it would take a little time.

Coming back late one evening, Sachiko sensed something of a commotion in the upstairs rooms. She didn't want to intrude but nevertheless should take a look out of concern.

Saeko sat on her low chaise longue – imported from Paris all those years before – and with one hand she gently petted Mozart. Oh, my boy, my boy, my baby, baby boy, she cooed. Oh, I know you are confused. You think that Mummy really birthed you don't you, and now you want to be my lover!

Sachiko was pleased she'd refrained from speaking, but she knew she wouldn't be able to retreat without being seen and so took a breath and opted for a friendly evening greeting as though she hadn't heard a thing. Saeko had a small glass nearby. It was empty. Mozart and Clementine were at Sachiko's ankles in a flash wanting to say hello. They jumped as high as they could. As Sachiko crouched down to greet them, Saeko let out a roar accompanied by the small glass hurled in their direction. Both dogs squealed but it was Sachiko's shin that took the hit.

The little dogs were deceitful, disloyal, didn't deserve their mommy who spoiled them! Saeko raged. Sachiko snatched a breath and placed her hand on her leg. Mozart and Clementine hid. You little shits! Both of you! Why don't you just run off with her if she's so adorable? You little shits, run away with this bitch!

Sachiko scanned the shadows to try and make out where the dogs had taken refuge. Nowhere to be seen. She tried to reassure herself that that was for the best. Saeko's outbursts were clearly not rare, it seemed the little dogs knew where to escape to. Saeko had quietened. Sachiko took tiny backward steps and barely breathed until she reached the top of the stairs. She turned and gently stepped downstairs. This was not good. Not good at all.

In the morning at school a parcel was delivered in her name and on it a small handmade card. From Kaori. She had wanted to thank her friend for all her help with the shop and celebrate Sachiko's new chapter in finally finding a nice home. It was the chamomile dress. Sachiko had tears in her eyes as she opened it. It was too generous, it was so lovely and it had been made with thought and skill and love. The card read that she should fill the pockets with her wishes for the future. Sachiko knelt down and one of the little girls came and rested a little hand on her knee and asked what was wrong. Sachiko shouldn't show her tears to the children even if they were happy ones. She wiped her eyes and took the little girl's hand, they would read a story soon. They ought to choose the book.

Sachiko sent a thank you message to Kaori. She knew from experience that when things were hardest you had to be your toughest, your most resilient. Moving in with this stranger had been a mistake. Moving again would be difficult. The fewer possessions you had the easier moving could be. Throughout her day with the children she snatched brief moments between activities to calculate just how little you needed, just how much you had to keep in order to just get by. And every time she did this she subtracted things from the list. She would repeat, like a mantra, something her grandfather had always said when she was little:

all you have is who you are
and who you are must be enough

In the light of not having a reliable long-term plan, she would opt for time by the sea, a couple of days. For rest, for recovery. Enoshima. The island was an easy train ride from Tokyo, she knew the journey well and the fare was cheap. She was owed a few days holiday and the kindergarten had recently taken on someone new. She would secure some days and message Kaori that she was taking some time by the sea. She wouldn't give more details just yet, it wasn't necessary to worry her. And besides, was there need for worry?

all you have is who you are
and who you are must be enough

She chanted the words in her mind to give her the courage to do this.

She was granted the time away despite a few raised eyebrows at the kindergarten at the very short notice; and she endeavoured to keep appearances cheery, nothing untoward, nothing for anyone else to care about, just a few days by the sea.

Her heart pounded as she returned to the house that evening. It was normal now that she had no idea what scene might greet her on entry. All she knew was that she must bear it, just as the little dogs had to. In the morning, Sachiko feigned feeling unwell and told Saeko she would be staying at home. Saeko suspected nothing but warned her not to let the dogs out, they might never come back if they were to get out. Sachiko promised to be very careful and Saeko set off to wherever she worked. Sachiko took a breath.

She packed a small backpack and put on the yellow dress. She stepped from the house as though what she was doing was quite the right thing. All you have is who you are, and what Saeko was, was not enough.

When she had walked far enough that she felt she wouldn't be discovered, she stopped a moment and allowed herself to breathe properly. She chanted to herself:

> all you have is who you are
> and that's quite enough
> – Mozart and Clementine in my pockets.

Mrs Murata

It's taken me a very long time and such a lot of work, but I have delighted in this so much. – Where we live in the far north of Honshu, so many people have left. Off, to Tokyo! Off, to find their fortunes abroad! That sort of thing. They used to come back. It was always accepted, the younger generation would go off and study, try their luck in the city. But always, always, they came back. They would come home married, or come home and marry and take up a position in the family profession very often. Raise a beautiful family.

I used to work on the maternity ward when I was younger. Oh those babies. Those beautiful, beautiful babies. Proud parents. Honoured grandparents, even great grandparents. All those people, all those ages. Like flowers at different stages, budding, blooming, withering – well, let's not talk about that part.

So you see, this place, it emptied out! They stopped returning. They stopped returning and stopped returning and stopped returning…

It was lucky for me that I had given up working. It would have broken my heart to see that maternity ward empty. Completely empty, I was told. No mothers. No babies. Then the staff were gone too. Can't run a maternity ward without pregnancies. Just a ghost ward. Cobwebs lacing the cribs where covers used to lay. And those that could bear children, long gone. No young men here anymore, no young women. No sex! No sex... well, perhaps some, but none that would produce a child.

The streets emptied, the cafes, the bus stops stood with nobody waiting. And the schools! No babies means no young children. No children and the teachers leave.

I had joked with the priest at our temple once that the cemetery was fast becoming the most populated place. I made him laugh, but we each had a tear. And that was it, that was the moment and I knew something must be done. I would bring people, I would fill the houses and the shops and the bus shelters, the schools and... anyway, now at least, I had somewhere to start.

It really took some time, but I soon upped my pace. I had to think about who the people should be, and how many of each kind, and I had to consider their hearts and minds so as to inform their expressions. Eventually I realised that each should be unique.

Years. I have spent years at this. But now when you walk about the town you find people everywhere. It had always been an interest of mine, knitting, but this was on an industrial scale. When I finished the first full grown adults and what looked like a teenager, I planted them at the bus stop. In the afternoon it clouded over and so I ran and gathered them and placed them inside the bus shelter. Sitting and standing. Huddled together. They were so very grateful, hugging me and offering their thanks. I told them it was nothing, but it touched my heart that I had helped them.

38

At the school these days, I see the youngsters sitting upright neatly. I peer through a window and don't want to interrupt their studies. I'm so proud of them. Their manners, their cheerful faces. At times I hear them sing for recently they have started choir practice. That rather fills my heart. If my husband were still alive I'm sure he'd tease me, but he knows how much I always loved the children. The children and the babies. We weren't blessed. But I feel blessed now.

Arthritis in both hands. But it doesn't much matter. Everyone is here now. They all came back, and I know that they'll look after me. You can't knit a village. That's what he would say. My husband. They won't be real. But deep down he knew that he was wrong.

Mr Seki

An old man lived at the corner of their street. He was a widower, had been some time. A sweet old man but they didn't see him outside anymore. How long had it been? Might be several years even. A neighbour, yet they had never actually introduced themselves. The house on the corner was perhaps just a little too far away, one house too far to invite the precise-imprecise feeling of neighbourly, though they might recognise one another on the street those years before, when his wife was still alive. Then, of course, they would all bow cordially and exchange appropriate greetings. But never quite stopping for a chat. Just that one house too far along.

He had dementia now. Had had for some time. Most likely. People weren't sure, the people thereabouts, but they speculated that that was probably the case. Yes. Most likely. That would be why he wasn't seen anymore. What a shame. There were towns they had read about that placed bar codes on those with dementia, that if an elderly person who could not be readily identified seemed lost, they could be scanned. Returned. Scanned and returned, yes, that's how it was. So they said. Perhaps some wouldn't like that, wouldn't want to be returned. Or scanned. Nevertheless. Nevertheless.

And then there was a middle-aged man who lived across town in Shibuya. Shibuya, the young people's domain. He had long since outgrown it. The hours imposed on him at work had curtailed his youth. Job instability, market instability, instability facing uncertainty. And sleep. So little of that. Not a moment even to masturbate. Nor the will. And women? No. Men? No. But the man at the Izakaya knew his face. Knew his face, the crown of his head over small dishes. Seven beers. Sake. And slumped. Round shoulders guiding him back. And the weekend. Saturday at the office. Things to finish up. As usual. Not obligatory and yet, expected? Um.. and… and then Sunday. Cross the city. To visit his father. A widower. Quite alone. The dementia was all now. Scattered thoughts, lost remembrances. He should help him shave but the old man hit out at him, pushed him away. Who was the younger man? A thief? A knife in his hand! Your son, I am your son, *Shunsuke. Shunsuke, Father.* I want to trim that beard. You favour being clean shaven. *Get away! Get away, you thief! You frighten me.*

The son cooks. The father spits. Then shits. The son pours some sake, they each take a sip. The father is baffled, embarrassed. Sobs. The son cleans him up. Puts on fresh clothes. Pyjamas now, it's late. The son washes the other clothes. Hangs them up on the veranda. Distant neighbours observe his movements. They note his weekly visits. But they do not know him.

First thing Monday morning, the start of a very new week, the son takes a different route to the office. This time from his father's home. In the evening he will return with shopping, the weekly supplies and cook and leave all, hoping that the old man might manage. Until Sunday. He will come again then. When? On Sunday, Father. Sunday. And over. And repeat. And again.

That night, half-moon in the sky, tipping as though it might fall. The young man left open the windows after putting more washing out on the veranda. His cries were audible and carried down the street. *Just fucking die I tell you!* I just want you to die and give me some peace. Just give me back my life! *Please, just die now and give me back my life.* Shunsuke sobbed into his hands. The old man was bewildered. He placed his hand gently on his son's head, a head he did not recognise and he stroked it in the manner of those who meet with a cat that has strayed inside.

Oh, dear me, don't cry, don't cry, the old man said, and he patted the man so kindly, and so gently, your family will be missing you, we must get you home to them, home to bed, young man, and soon.

Misaki

It started during the pandemic. I think. This change in me. Yes. It did. Though in some ways the pandemic made no difference at all to the event, things alter a person's mind, but it truly might have gone like this anyway. For me, maybe COVID-19 was just the final necessary impetus for what I thought of as: *gotta make shit happen*. Anyway, the pandemic, that's when this took place.

I was quite new to the area, it was pretty and rural. My parents were in Tokyo. Professionals: lawyer, dentist. Essential but ugly professions. I quit my own studies in dentistry, afraid I'd lose my mind, my soul. Maybe I'd open a café out here, I had money, and access to money, and access to this and that if I wanted to continue my existence as an asshole, taking and taking, but I had high hopes I could be better than that. A better person. Not sure how to judge that to be honest, and the ways things turned out.

I took over a small dwelling with a meagre patch of land. I watched and learned from neighbours, distantly took advice, masked of course. I learned to grow stuff, fix stuff, and it seemed I was rather handy at both.

Being outside felt like a good fit, the air, the soil, the partial isolation or at least the distance afforded the non-dental from the gaping mouths of others. People didn't take too badly to the girl moved up from the city – it seemed. At first. In any case, I was always quizzed and criticised the hell out of for taking up dentistry studies. A man's profession. Nursing was more acceptable, and I am so past that bullshit. Fuck acceptable!

I had a neighbour, an older man, and he seemed to live alone. Not friendly at all but I found that amusing. I like people who don't really need other people, that emotional self-sufficiency isn't far from me. Sometimes I like people, but whether or not I need them is still up for question. I mean: I can do it, socialising, all the normal interaction, but it feels like an act. The act of being human, an act of being human, approximating. After all, despite not going the whole way, who the hell even goes into dentistry? There's something dark about it. I think I was cautious about that, being dark, perhaps becoming more dark, forever in a mask, tools to hand. And the drilling. Oh my. So, I was wise. I left that crap behind me.

Out here, closer to the natural world I might study plant life, indigenous species, all kinds of creatures. And perhaps I would get a telescope. The sky was clearer up here in the mountains; what far away stars might I see now? I would build a tower for this too. Observation. Nice plan.

When you are eccentric, you don't know it. People say it of you, very rarely to you and it's akin to being ill in the head I believe. That's how I heard my old man neighbour describing me one early afternoon. Not Covid-19, she's just sick in the head. Well, there we are, I thought. I shrugged and carried on digging. I would make some good and sturdy base for the observation tower. It might need to be concrete. That would be a first for me if that was the case. But I was up for it. Much to consider.

An old woman brought out some tea and laughed with me at my great ambition. I told her she was welcome to come try it out when I had completed the build. She blushed and chortled and withdrew. People, I can't read them, but anyway.

There seemed to be a lot of stray animals in the area, moved in when they were abandoned at the start and during the pandemic, would be my guess. But my guess is usually 'off', people often say.

The tower went through various incarnations. At first people didn't want to help but when they saw how rickety the structure was they came good. I'd never built big before, just small cupboards and that type of thing. Just learning on the hoof, and always quite slowly. I was a careful worker. Anyway, the tower needed making safe, and so with the neighbours' reluctant help, it got made. I understood, it was the pandemic, people needed distance. I needed distance, pandemic or no, that's why I was there. But the tower needed to come into being, and absolutely right then because, no, I couldn't be patient and wait until the disease had passed. What the hell? This entire project was in order to keep my sanity. I had to get it made.

It was a good feeling to eat the vegetables I had grown myself. I lacked meat but was trying to go vegetarian. Not sure it was wise. I got thin. Maybe wasn't doing it right.

The old man neighbour spied on me quite a lot it. Perhaps I imagined some portion of that, shadows, the shadow of something else, someone else. I tried to figure it in a way that didn't disturb me. I wanted to see the stars in the distance, he wanted to observe a young person's endeavours, that type of thing. Probably nothing untoward. It was my hope that he was impressed by my labours. I laughed out loud at that, embarrassed, for sure there was little to admire in my craftwork and building, but shit, I was giving it my best shot.

In the evenings I studied about the stars, readying myself. I had cut contact with my family by now. They didn't get me at all. Well, I had little need of being understood, but nonetheless I was grateful that they still wanted to fund me. If I was anyway decent I wouldn't accept their money. Well, that's another thing I have to work on. Emotions and a conscience seemed hard for someone like me to conceive of. I glibly wondered whether they were things I could download some place. I know, I am rude. Always hard for the world to accept character imperfections in women. The bar is set too high, I tell you. Too fucking well high. So screw it all. So little is expected of men by comparison, that's why some of them murder. Isn't it? Not many women do that. Actually, I don't know. How would I know? It's just what I think, just as an ordinary member of society.

This is what happens. When I don't keep busy. I just ruminate, ruminate and ruminate. And all of it is useless. No grand conclusions.

So, back to work. And the tower. Should I paint it? A step too far? It could be rather cheerful looking out here in say yellow or orange, but perhaps the natural colour of the wood is enough in its green surroundings.

Tiny frogs had gathered around my feet whilst I stood there musing, a real troupe and when I lifted my foot they moved with me. I stepped again and this continued. What were they doing? No matter, it felt strangely comforting. And I had no idea I was in need of comfort. I shrugged my shoulders. I liked the frogs. A lot.

And so the tower came into being. If I been one for celebrations I suppose I'd have opened some special alcohol, but I never drank and I didn't know what else to do. That was fine. When I got to see the stars, that would be my celebration.

As I climbed up, slowly and mindful of my footing, I heard a rustling some place behind me. I looked over my shoulder but couldn't see anything out of the ordinary. I carried on, pausing a moment to check my feet and catch my breath. The wind was up. The structure seemed to creak, but my weight couldn't be too much. Of late I was nothing but bone. I was caused to look down, never wise when climbing, and I didn't know what drew me to do it, but when I did, there he was. The old man neighbour, gripping the bottom of one of the struts. Never a word between us, but now he seemed to want to help as though holding a ladder for a friend. There was truly no need, the structure, I was confident, was really quite fine. Of course, it was narrow, the proportions modest, it was a tower just for one, but it did not require a grown adult to steady it, kind as it seemed. I stemmed my natural urge to read it as his criticism of my ability to construct such a thing, but no, he was genuinely worried for my safety. He was simply over cautious. I tilted my head as a means of thanking him, but I doubted he would hear if I called out. Unmasked, he seemed to move his mouth but nothing, no idea what he said. Take care, was my guess.

The tower seemed to give a little, and I sensed I needed to compensate and adjust my position. When you are about to fall, everything slows down. I read about this absently at university, why or how the brain takes us through a traumatic event in slow motion – something about allowing us a sense of extra time to take in the details, thus possibly allowing another part of the brain to find a nice solution. Is that what I read? I may have invented it as my own sweet myth to help me out, right about now.

As I fall I sense my back arching. I become a crescent moon. Still, everything is in slow mo. The wind travels past me in straight lines, I peer up trying to make myself believe I can see far-away stars with my bare eyes. The old man is there. What has he done?

I landed with a thud, I felt it through my torso. My neck had twisted. I was gone.

The old man neighbour, took up his axe. He hacked off my feet. Left the rest of me where I lay. He walked some distance, my feet in his hands. On a hill he dug two shallow grooves, placed a foot in each. He placed a wooden sign right by them.

WOMEN MUST KEEP THEIR FEET ON THE GROUND.

Since then, I spend my time, up here, up here with the stars.

I visit the old man neighbour on the hour every hour as my ghost. I am his dentist. He must have his teeth pulled. All are rotten. Over and again. I am a dentist, his dentist. Not entirely trained.

Mr Takahashi

I have a family, of course. A wife, and two children now grown up. It is fair to say that each of us goes our own way. My wife has her life about which I know very little, but she is certainly happy enough. My children, one girl, one boy, are naturally fully provided for and have always been. They are both at extremely good universities and since neither is particularly bright, they should be grateful for all my connections. Fortunately, I never needed such favours, but I am happy that I can facilitate my offspring.

I am the head of a very powerful company and in my younger days worked very long hours. I doubt very much that my own son would be able to cope with anything close. So, let's see what becomes of him. One can only hope at this stage.

As I progress in years, so my status grows, my salary, and my appetites for things other than work goals. This seems very natural to me. I have served my time, so to speak, now for the rewards. Although I am almost sixty years of age my physique is strong and athletic and I would say it is closer to that of a man some twenty years my junior. I feel this to be of benefit to myself and to others. Very much.

My schedule nowadays is such that I can fit in rather more golf than before, longer lunches and there is some further negotiable timetabling that enables the satiation of other necessities. I found in recent years, for example, that I am partial to something more than just a trim when I go to have my hair tidied up. I now enjoy making the most of my appearance – *as suggested by the salon staff* – and have a facial with some regularity, including a deep facial massage using Swiss products. It is almost an obligation nowadays to look your best, particularly for someone in a senior position such as my own, and standards are always rising. It is no longer merely the duty and privilege of movie stars. And although initially reluctant, I now see immeasurable value in eyebrow shaping and note that it does in fact enhance my handsome eyes. Again, the staff commented as much, I merely repeat their observation. And I also agree with them that altogether this frames the face. – I have heard these treatments are commonplace in Italy and France and they are to be much admired. Men of stature. Because, although I am not exactly *in* politics, there is a certain level of business that is almost equal in status and it appears that this is a category that has chosen men such as myself.

For some time now, I have had a girlfriend. She is eighteen and was just fifteen when we met. Naturally, as a good and decent man, I waited some time for things to develop into the anticipated sexual expression of our mutual affection. In the meantime we would meet about two, maybe three times a week at what became our secret hideaway, our special bar.

To show my appreciation of my girlfriend's femaleness, I always bought her gifts. Of course she would try not to accept them, such was her manner, and this only endeared her to me all the more. It was a long time since I had encountered this particular female politeness, this delicacy, and it gave me a similar joy to the experience of the finest sushi. In such cases it is difficult to be sated. I feel a sense of hunger that I have to stem.

Eventually, she could resist me no more, I tease, but actually that is truly what she said, and our relationship became physical. It was, an awakening for me. It was like transferring in one's gastronomic taste from good sushi, to the most exquisite sashimi. You can imagine my joy.

During this time, both my own children naturally moved away to have their own lives. I think my wife may have felt a kind of empty nest syndrome, but on the other hand her work was done, and she could now relax into old age without cares. I considered what a fortunate life she had lived. And now when I was at home she was busily engaged in handicrafts, making small things, I don't know what to be honest, but cute things. I was lucky in that she was not the greedy kind of spouse, she managed our accounts very well, and rarely bought things for herself, no extravagant tastes. In fact, in the past we had joked about how it was me who was apt to spend and how I needed reigning in. My own private extravagance of having a lover went unnoticed as I continued to use cash and explained it away as business expenses. After all, that is what men do. And I was glad never to have to worry that I had a wife who over spent or liked expensive brands. I basked in the knowledge of her thrifty housekeeping. By contrast, a colleague of mine privately named his wife, Gucci-wife, and he worried terribly about their future retirement. Nothing was ever further from my mind. My wife had everything in hand, a great saver, even something of an expert I would think. I admired her. A good wife all in all.

Well, enough of that. But quite soon after my relationship deepened with my girlfriend, I encountered an American man, a peer so to say, in an industry related to my own. Super smart and I would also add that I found him very charismatic. Safe to say I have never liked a man more. Alongside spending time with my girlfriend, I made sure to make time for this guy while he stayed in Japan. He thought his stay was likely to be some three months with the possibility of extending this, and I soon very much hoped that this would be the case.

We spent many a night swapping stories together over beer and sake and I enjoyed his take on many things, in fact he is perhaps the most refreshing person I have ever met. He would talk devotedly about his family, and like me, had a boy and a girl. But unlike me, the family sounded very close, as though they were friends, true and real friends. I found this charming and I think that gradually I envied him this. How was it like that? How are you truly good friends with a son, with a daughter? Why was he so involved in their lives? Visiting them often at university, sharing in their interests so deeply. I also found it a little strange to be honest. How did he have time? Was he lying? At least exaggerating this super family life? Had to be. For a time I wanted to believe that and then enjoyed thinking ill of him. And yet it seemed to have been the case, they were always messaging and making video calls, including with his wife, even interrupting my conversations with him! I joked that he would get lonely in Japan without them and he nodded, so, I suggested that like me, he find himself a girlfriend. He frowned and then laughed. A laugh that was clearly put on. I took it that he was a shy guy in that respect and might need the benefit of my broader experience. Well, it was best to take it slowly. Not all men are confident with women.

Some nights later he asked me if I really had a girlfriend. Of course! So, I took this as an expression of interest and gently offered to see if I would be able to introduce him to someone. He took offence. And this time the uncomfortable laughter was on my side. He told me he was not that way inclined, that he was a family man. Well, I'm a family man myself, so this made no sense. I was now also offended. *What the hell!* I remained silent then for some time and then ordered some very good sake, especially good. I had meant no harm and wanted to smooth things over.

Despite his insistence that he was not interested himself he ventured to ask me a number of personal questions. How I had met my girlfriend, was my wife aware and accepting – *how ridiculous, of course not* – what age was the girl, what was the nature of our relationship? I could not have imagined that this level of inquisition could be made by any other than a deeply interested party. And stupidly, I answered him freely, thinking I was perhaps assisting him in overcoming some heavy shyness in these matters. Needless to say, I was wrong. So wrong. He challenged me and scoffed when I mentioned her age and the gifting I had engaged in which he laughing called the lavish work of a *fool old man*. Though I may have misheard, it is really too offensive to speak that way. Totally, utterly.

We drank and we drank and finally, after several more video call interruptions, he suggested that my girlfriend was unlikely to be in love with me, something I had confided in him. She had said this to me numerous times. I love you, I love you and even in French, *je t'aime!* He insisted it was extremely unlikely that she did, love me, and suggested I stop buying gifts for her the next few times to test this out. I took the challenge. If there was a fool here it wasn't me. My girlfriend had not been with me all this time for presents and money. He scoffed again. It was fine, I would take his test.

We decided that three appointments with my girlfriend would be a good amount. Each time I met up with her I was permitted to give her nothing at all, no special gift and no gift of money. And I was to check her reaction and behaviour in response.

The first time got me worried, I have to admit – she looked so disappointed when I showed up emptyhanded. I almost gave up on the challenge, after all, was it worth upsetting her just to prove a point. But by the end of our delicious lovemaking she seemed happy, running her finger around the nape of my neck and cooing softly. Next time, she said.

On the second encounter, she thought that I was teasing her, for why had I brought her nothing? She pulled out my wallet and tugged at the notes, but I calmly and firmly took it back and gently but resolutely told her, not today. She smiled at me and recovered her mood well. We did not have sex but chose instead to take a nice walk as she wanted to look at the moon.

On the third visit she was absent, and on the fourth and fifth. She blocked my phone number. I had never known her address. I was deeply saddened. So, so deeply.

I met with the American. He had won, I told him but he wasn't interested. Wasn't interested. Not in anything with me anymore, it was clear, not anymore. He yawned, paid our bill and left early.

I wandered at no pace back home. My wife would be there. Familiarity, that was what was needed. Even just the comfort of seeing her face. For the first time ever I was overcome with guilt at my betrayal. I had never thought like that before. Nothing close. The things in my world were separate, the things in my life held different meanings. Different also to the American's. I wasn't wrong, he wasn't right, he wasn't a better man than me. Video calling his children and wife every two minutes like a child himself. I got home and stood a moment by the door taking in the air, breathing, just breathing. Appreciating my life and all that I had. All that I was. I entered the house quietly, it was late, took off my shoes and searched in the dark for slippers. I was smiling to myself. I was happy. I called out in a quiet voice hoping my wife was still awake. We would have a late night sake together or a tea. We didn't usually, but tonight, tonight it would be nice. There was no response. I switched on the main light. I blinked a couple of times. Empty. Every last stick, gone. And my wife, gone. I swung around from room to room. My head began to throb. In a small woven basket that she had made, I found a note. I read it. I moved about the house again. My eyes filled up. Silly sentimental man. I sat down at the entrance and took a cigarette. '*Now I take my life back. Goodbye.*' That's all it said. Just that. Nothing more. Nothing more, no more, no more of anything, nothing at all. Gone now. Nothing. I looked back again. Not even a spider.

Hiromichi

I've known times of struggle in the past myself. When I was a student briefly in Chicago, I fell upon hard times and genuinely thought I might find myself homeless. I don't like to think about it. I'm back home and things have sorted themselves out. It's actually really hard to pull back the details, stuff I went through abroad, but I have a sense of it sometimes and it always makes me shiver. Like being taken by surprise by your own shadow when you change direction suddenly, rounding a corner or the light changing when clouds shift. A horrible, disconcerting feeling. And more than that.

In Japan, I feel safe again, it's home. I have a few people here that I can rely on and realise now just how much I need them. I work as an illustrator – children's books mostly. It's nice work and recently I've been sharing some modest studio space with another artist. It's made all the difference as my own place is also on the small side. It feels so good not to be cooped up in my small apartment while I draw. I like the quiet company of the other artist, Akiko. She has a calm disposition too and it suits me to be around her. We give each other peace and quiet, space I guess, to get the work done and then we have a coffee or discuss our projects over a simple lunch. We are almost like monks. It's quite funny. Cute even. – The best thing is that I can now eke out a living. – Anyway, to my story:

when I was coming back home two nights ago I passed a guy curled up in an odd position on the street, he didn't look comfortable at all. I didn't like to assume he was homeless, but it was cold and the forecast said that the temperature would drop further in the night. I got closer and said something casual and then I realised that he wasn't Japanese. I switched to English but he didn't answer very quickly so I worried. I don't know any other languages. I stood a moment blowing air into my hands and he finally looked up. He said he was OK. I felt relieved, he did speak English, good; so I squatted down, careful in case he was drunk or something but actually he was fine. I smiled and said it was cold, too cold to be outdoors like this. He nodded. From his face and clothes I couldn't really work out much about him. His accent wasn't familiar to me either. At the same time, I know people are sometimes upset when you ask a lot of personal things, where they're from and so on, so I thought best not to ask too much. He didn't move. I motioned to him to get up and suggested that if he came with me, my place was close by now, I could make him some hot tea. I thought he was around my age, perhaps a little older.

He came along with me in a rather indifferent manner. I didn't feel worried at all about inviting him. Not at all. He was someone in need and to be honest I was more than happy, maybe even overly eager to help. Sometimes people abroad had shown me tremendous kindness. I wanted to do the same.

As we entered my home I realised I had been chatting away to him the whole time, I don't even know about what. I apologised and found him some slippers, showing him that he should take off his shoes. He seemed reluctant to take them off, or perhaps he'd become stiff from sitting in the cold so long. That's happened to me before now, often actually, when I sit and draw too long without realising and the limbs seize up.

I made some hot soup for us. It took some time in preparation as I wanted to use all fresh ingredients and cook from scratch, give him something wholesome and warming. He complained that I was taking too long, which took me by surprise to be honest. And when I came from the kitchen to speak to him he laughed very heartily at my apron. I was taken aback by his reaction, and yet I felt it was good to have helped him cheer up, however unintentionally. I was rather conflicted.

He mumbled rather a lot and I struggled to follow what he said. But he seemed to be enjoying the soup. I asked if he had a place to stay, he replied that he had not or I wouldn't have found him lying on the street. I asked if he knew anyone here, and he responded similarly. Then I grew nervous of making any further enquiries. I had no need to pry, and I was not in the game of trying to make another person feel uncomfortable about their life or situation, I merely wanted to understand what was going on with him so that I could help. And I worried someone might be looking for him or waiting for him. But by now I guessed not.

He asked for more soup, I gave him some and felt pleased that he liked it. He noticed some sketches of mine about the place, and asked under his breath, what were they for? They were some rough fox drawings I was working on, a new idea for a children's book, I told him. I saw his eyes lighten and flicker and a little colour grew in his cheeks. I gathered the pictures together and placed them near him, bidding him to take a closer look if he should like to. It was my original idea, and I explained how I generally worked from a writer's story, how this was fine, but that someday I would like things to happen the other way around: start with my artwork and let the writer find words later. He passed up his empty bowl and asked if he might wash his hands before handling the paper. I was touched. He knew to treat an artist's work with respect. I pointed to the tiny bathroom and casually uttered, please, help yourself. I fumbled around for a clean towel for him. Now, he truly was my guest I felt.

When he came out I withdrew to the kitchen under the pretence of washing the dishes. I didn't want to be in the room when he perused my work. Suddenly shy.

I heard a shuffling. What was he doing? Fidgeting noises. Perhaps he was just making himself comfortable. I called, asking, did he need anything? Beer, he responded. Get me a beer. Just that, abrupt, clear. When a man knows precisely his need it seems he can find his voice. OK, and a part of me was amused by this, perhaps even a little impressed. Well, not so much impressed, but somewhat entertained. As I opened the can I hoped I had never behaved in the same way. I took another beer for myself.

With the fresh advantage of the beer to offer him, I ventured to ask a few things. I gave him the can and he asked for a glass as though I was offending him, treating him like a brute. I retreated to the kitchen and returned with two glasses. He looked at me for a moment and gave a heavy nod. I have no idea what he intended to communicate in this but it felt a little awkward. I drank deeply on my beer then asked rather quickly, what was his name, where was he from, had he been in Japan very long? He continued to stare at my works and did not reply.

So, he said, this is what you do? For a living, you draw? You have a good eye. And these are for books. That's a nice life. Few people get to do that. - I was flattered and excited to be indulged like this and impressed he knew anything at all about my profession. I told him as much but he responded darkly, that he was not an idiot.

Foxes are interesting, he said, adding, and so are cats. He scanned the room as though looking for one. I told him I didn't have a pet. He looked disappointed in me. Indeed, I felt, disappointed in me. It would be nice to have a pet, would make all the sense in the world to have one. And yet, I did not. They are good company, I offered, pets: cats, dogs. He nodded, supped on his beer, smiled mischievously and said, he knew that cats and dogs were pets. I drank more of my beer. His character was not easy.

Will you let me stay here? He asked, placing my artwork carefully to one side. My eyes followed his hands. My heart wondered why he had not commented further on my drawings. But he had shown a generous interest, taking a look, washing his hands in advance and he handled the pages with great care. All of this I witnessed and appreciated. Could you get me another beer, he added, taking off his sweater. Without thinking I responded automatically to his request and fetched more beer. He asked if the futon he spied was spare and lay himself down on it. I had been about to say, yes. I placed the beer near to him but already he was sleeping. I felt a deep sense of compassion towards him. Imagine, being so very tired. I would let him sleep.

I shuffled some things about and lay down rather near to him as my place did not really permit anything more comfortable or polite. He smelt of herbs when I expected he might just smell rather dirty. Curious. Not drugs, just light smelling herbs, perhaps rosemary. I wondered, was it perfume?

When I awoke, the man was still sleeping. I did not like to disturb him, and for a moment I was concerned, I lent near to make sure that I could hear him breathing. He was alive. I felt happy. I dressed quickly for work and laid out a few simple things on a tray for his breakfast, and placed them close to his head. I left, and as I walked I considered that though in some small sense he was comfortable to be around, I had no idea really of anything about him. I shrugged. When I got to work I would tell Akiko.

One of the first things Akiko wanted to know was, what the hell, her actual words, in English too, 'What the hell..' was I doing taking in strangers, letting them sleep over, and leaving them unattended in my place? She was right, of course. But I didn't like her tone. I didn't answer her and got on with my work. By the end of the day I had all but forgotten that I had

had a guest. I had purposefully left my door unlocked (this area is safe) so that he could leave easily, and I wondered what might have happened to him this day.

When I got home he was still there. Almost unrecognisable as he had clearly bathed, shaved and was dressed in a pair of my own pyjamas. I was obviously surprised. I think I was both delighted and.. and what? Astounded, I suppose, by his impertinence. Never in my life would I behave like that, just helping myself. However, I had to remember, that placed in situations of adversity, people do behave outside the normal range of acceptable behaviours. Before I could speak, he asked if I had brought home dinner. And beers, we were out of beers. No, I responded. I had not. His eyes were not unkind and bid me go get what might be needed. I have no idea why I was so obedient in his presence but I was. I took a moment to divest myself of my work bag, and take a glass of water, so as not to appear too much in awe and under his spell, and then I set out again to get groceries for our supper. It was as though I was a child again. And I have no idea why I found this quite so amusing, for sure I would not be telling Akiko, but it did amuse me. Was I such a masochist? It appeared, at least in this brief time, that I enjoyed being bossed around. I learned something new about myself.

It was an entire week that we lived together this way, we would eat and share beers, he would look at some of my work. His interest in me would distract from the fact that I had no idea who he was, where he came from, what were his intentions. I never mentioned him again to Akiko and allowed her to believe he had simply stayed the one night with me and that it was a kind of foolish gesture on my part. But each day I would return home and find him in my clothes waiting for me to feed him. It struck me how like a cat he was. It also struck me how arrogant his behaviour was, how passively and innocently he had inveigled himself. I was astonished when I took my walk to work each morning at just how smoothly this situation had appeared to set itself up. But so it was. And somehow I didn't seem to mind.

When a week had passed, I came home with a gift of take-away food, and better beers, as though I would celebrate something with my friend. I entered my place and he was gone. It was easy to check that he wasn't there as the place is so small, no need to call out, and also, I still had no idea of his name. There was a smell, a scent. Lemons. He had left a note. He was deeply grateful for the care and love I had shown a stranger. And lacking any other means of thanking me, had cleaned my place using fresh lemons. That was indeed the scent. I had never heard of such a thing. 'I have cleaned your house with lemons' – I dropped to my knees on the tatami, letting the bags I carried fall away. Oh, how I cried. Where was he now? After some long moments and a howling deep from inside, I gathered myself. I hauled in some breath and then more but slowing down. I noticed then, my pictures, the foxes. Pulled them near, they were clean, intact, but some pages now were added. The story. His story. Just a few words in the finest hand-written script, on single loose pages, one to fit with each sketch. I could not read them for tears. I fell forwards, pushing my face into the tatami and howled again, into the ground. Never had I cried like that. Never in my life.

I read his words, in English though I knew that was certainly not even his first language, but it seemed clear he was a master. My little foxes, how he had animated them. He had made them true, given life to them and poetry.

I got up and ran outside, I could not call out for him without his name. But I looked and looked, ran back to the place where I had first encountered him. Of course, he was not there. I screamed a name inside that I did not even know. *Please, oh please, please, please,* come back to me, come back…

I walked. On and on. Back and to. As midnight approached I returned to my place. Though I knew he would not be there, and with all my heart I so wished that he was. Never, never would I forget him.

I had the words, ready now, for the fox book. But the author was unknown. And my home now, smelt of lemons.

Kaori

I have told him we have to leave this house. He doesn't understand. I hate it. I'm allergic to it. Its walls, its windows, the hallways, there's something here and it is making me ill. He argues that we have just moved here. I tell him that it's all the more reason to move again soon, before the children feel settled, before they are too attached at school, for they are bound to make friends quickly, they are wonderful and funny. They are kind. He reminds me that it took a long time to find such a big, elegant house. He reminds me I helped choose it. That I, in fact, chose and insisted upon it. Well, perhaps we don't need such a big house. Did I say that it was elegant? Did I? Perhaps I did. Perhaps I was just being polite. I do that. We both do that I suppose. We are polite people. We have polite children. We live, we always live… wherever we live, for we move a lot, and internationally, for we are international, in a polite neighbourhood. In polite society. We are part, of polite society.

What I want is a piano. I still play. And I played professionally before becoming quite so polite. Quite so, married. He will get me a piano. I can have a piano room in fact, then I will be happy. I will have my 'own thing'.

The piano arrived from Germany. It's in my piano room. My own thing, in my own room. But the walls are the same walls, and the windows, the hallways, and the smell of the place, it doesn't change. I open the windows to ventilate and to change the smell; he buys aromatic candles and incense. The children feel distant. They too, have their own thing, their own rooms. They have their own smell. And he, he has a smell.

He says I need a doctor.

I tell him, it's the house.

Get a doctor.

I tell him, it's the house.

And so, it is settled, we are moving. He's online, contacting agents. We can afford almost anything so it ought to be possible and soon, I really couldn't breathe anymore. In the meantime I would take a hotel room. There was a piano I could use in the lobby.

He has found somewhere. I will like it, it's a little further out, the air will be less polluted, it has a garden. It is gated. It will be even safer. We will grow lavender.

The boxes are being unloaded. I am overwhelmed by the commotion. I go to lie down. The children are out in the garden. They like it there and I hear laughter. He calls to me to come and help unpack for I will know where things go, where I want things to be. Well, I don't. The house is a stranger. I have no idea where things ought to be. – He has to go to work earlier now as he has further to travel, but I'll be fine here won't I, in this wonderful palace?

He smiles, and it's too wide. His eyes, sparkle. I don't want him to come to this room. I close my eyes to remove him. We ought to cook, celebrate our new home, and the children are starving. Surely not, I think to myself. We could eat out, he suggests. I tell him that *they* should do that and go and have fun, but I'm exhausted by the day's events and had better stay in bed.

The windows here are large. They let in the sun. I will order blinds.

He's away now. Business. Brussels. I told him to be sure to take a lot of masks. Very many masks. He might get delayed. – He calls, but I don't always manage to answer.

I have found a new doctor. He's concerned about symptoms. My condition. I should buy only organic food, I can order this online. I must cook only simple dishes, eat only small portions so that my body is not overworked.

He is back today, a new food order has just arrived; and the young woman from the store fixed all the blinds to the frames. Everywhere is clean. He has brought me flowers. Cut flowers. He is looking for a vase. Tulips. But they are multicoloured and I like white. In fact, I don't like cut flowers, not at all. It's not my taste. I prefer, just one, or just a few. I don't like the 'bunch' idea. They look scruffy, unruly, dumped in a vase. He says I should study traditional arranging. Make it a hobby. I should, have, hobbies. He says that. Like the other women do. Or I could make cookies, like the other mothers do. Or teach Japanese to small children.

He wants to buy paintings now, for the walls. But I won't have it. I like them white. I like them as they are. I communicate this by not responding. He buys time by suggesting that there is plenty of it. Time. And perhaps we can think about paintings and more decorative elements, and lamps, when we feel more settled in. Decorative elements. My skin itches. I scratch at my right arm. He asks me to stop. I should put some cream on it. I continue to scratch. He doesn't like the blinds. He says so. But then he attempts to retract this, adding he appreciates all the trouble I have gone to.

Well, I do not like the house. I hate the house. This house, that house! The one before, the one we might move to next that is here or there in *this* fabulous country or that. And here are the things I cannot say ever, to anyone – my truest, deepest feelings, that no mother can ever say: I do not like my children, I wish I'd never had them. I wish I'd had the courage not to marry. I wish, with all my might, that all I had in the world was a tiny place in which to stay, and my music. I wish, with every last part of me for that. Just a small place and a piano. But you can't go back. You cannot give back the children you gave birth to, you cannot un-tread the steps you have taken and taken willingly. You can't. But all I want is to live in a modest place in my own country, my home country, in my Japan. Just myself, and my own breath.

I can smell the scent of the sea as I step into it. No scented candles nor lavender, no desperate cut flowers. No more, the roles that I cannot fulfil. And it's so cold as I step further. My ears fill up. So very cold. Waves break over me. And there is nothing now. And it is glorious. Just a breath.

Shohei

It was strange and beautiful that we met. I don't know why I spoke to her. A line of words left me and fell in her direction. A bridge I suppose. And I didn't know if I spoke intending for her to hear or if in the last moment I might try to pull it all back. I remember, my fingers had been tight in a fist and I let them uncurl.

I'd leant against a wall but sat now at the other end of the bench. And it's not like me to speak to strangers, and not women, definitely not a woman from another country. Doesn't matter. Her name was Grace. Just imagine, having a name like that. Kind of serene. I started to smoke and she coughed. I shouldn't smoke, ever. I wanted to though. I wanted to. She coughed again and scowled a little. I apologised but at the same time I liked that I had caused a reaction. I didn't want to irritate, I just liked that her expressions changed freely. So natural. That's what I thought: she's more natural than I am, more natural than most Japanese people, maybe all of us. I took another long drag. She felt something, she could not help but let it show. I remember. I apologised again and put out the cigarette. My actions seemed selfish. But I wanted to be.

I told her I was a monk, a novice. Her eyes seemed to get bigger. I explained some details, but not too much. I stopped I think because my words didn't seem to be helping. She didn't seem to believe me and the information I gave didn't seem relevant. She was surprised at my English, that I spoke so fluently. Why not? Why wouldn't it be? I shrugged.

Her sensitivity made her easily uncomfortable. She said she hadn't meant to offend me. I blushed at this. I felt the colour, the blood. We were total strangers and yet she was careful of my feelings.

So there we were, her name was Grace and she was from England. She was studying architecture at university here. I was a novice monk but she didn't believe me. Actually, I didn't believe her either but I didn't say, just thought it was funny. You really have to be super smart to get into that particular uni. and I had never heard of anyone non-Japanese making it there. I felt sure someone would make a documentary about it if it were true, it was really that rare. At the same time, I questioned myself, I mean, what did I know, it might be more common than I realised. No matter, I decided to accept it, I didn't actually mind if it was true or not. Of course, after some time, it turned out that she genuinely was super smart, all of it was true! For me this was so cool, she was amazing. – She would write up her thesis in English and later get it translated. However, I have to admit that this last part seemed to me to be both brilliantly clever and at the same time totally lame, but I wasn't sure about things at that level. Maybe that was normal. But I thought she should know Japanese much better than she did, and she should write the thesis directly in Japanese herself. Finally, I settled that she was way ahead of me in most things except perhaps language. My English was really good and secretly, I was super proud of that.

It was late autumn already with the feeling that winter would come soon and it made it feel quite romantic to me. You have to wear lots of clothes of course, in those colder seasons, and I always think that looks cool on women, on everyone actually; and you sleep with many futons, drink hot sake. I do that a lot. And smoke, usually. Yeah, Grace, she looked cute in her hat and scarf. Wispy hair at the edges of her green felt hat. You notice things and yet you try not to. I guess everyone does that.

We had started to meet up regularly, though each time was really brief as my schedule was hard. I would tell her that and tell myself that too, but I'm not sure that it was entirely honest. I wasn't sure if her studies were demanding for her, I think it was mostly research, and I don't know why but I never really asked that much about it. But it felt important to me to appear busy.

I had no proof, but I sensed that she liked me. And that felt so nice. And I liked being the one who had to dash away. That's also selfish, but anyway.

She said that I seemed unusual, untypical for a Japanese guy. Well, for sure I was, I was going to be a monk, that's not the most common thing to be. But she also found me rather insular and didn't like it when I didn't always respond. She said that she couldn't always read me. Then it was me who was uncomfortable. I wasn't really OK with that. What does it mean to read someone, why do you need to make this close scrutiny, why do you need to reveal so much all the time? But

I suppose some people need to wear everything on the out-side, thoughts, opinions. Your inner-most thoughts wriggling all over your face. Anyway, that's not my style and not my way. I remember I shrugged in response. Then I smiled, aware that I might seem rude. That kind of discussion was a little complicated.

She called me enigmatic. I was sure this was good but I had to check it in the dictionary later just to be certain. When I read the definition it was like getting a big compliment all over again. I had to have a cigarette to calm myself. And it had made me feel greedy. Strange. And good. I wanted more. I don't think I was used to being liked that much. Just a more ordinary level is fine for me to be honest.

She would ask me about my future. I joked about how right now I didn't even want to think about it. I have to be a monk, I told her. Now I am just a novice, almost a *novice* novice, because I am actually a student of history right now and later I will study Buddhism more deeply and then go to the moun-tains for further study. My words seemed to unsettle her. Perhaps what you say can seem less like the truth when you speak too honestly. I don't know. But I thought it was the right thing to do. Be totally clear about my situation. Misunderstanding might be prevented that way. Of course, I told her I could marry, it's possible inside Japanese Buddhism, I made sure to tell her that. She seemed surprised. I don't really know why I said it, it's just a fact. It had been the farthest thing from my mind really. But maybe I wanted to seem less strange, mention a few of the more ordinary things that would still apply to my life despite my being a monk. Make me more relatable? I never thought about things like that normally. Not at all. I had some difficult things to deal with in my future, and not so many options up ahead. It was hard for me right at that time, to know and to accept that my future was decided, that I would not be a lawyer or an actor or any kind of activist or engineer or anything. I suppose I wanted to pretend to myself that some parts of my life were still open and not all a given, that I could still do some of the things that other people do. It's pretty tough foregoing choices.

Over time it turned out that Grace couldn't speak very much Japanese at all and so we always fell into English. She said again that I was good at languages and how that was rare since the Japanese are famously bad at them. This was too straight to be honest. When she talked like this it could really be awkward for me. Lots of opinions about so many things, spoken loud and clear. Just so straight. Too much. It was interesting but I didn't often have any words to say in reply. I would be quiet for a moment or I would smoke. That was normal in my case. Anyway, it was cool that she thought my English was good at least.

I often found it liberating talking to Grace, and exciting. It had this unreal quality. I told her how it felt like being in the movies or something, like a parallel existence. Never entirely real. Maybe hyper-real? I don't know. But with her I felt I could be a different me. Maybe that has a childish sound to it. But I felt so high when I spoke in English like that, with her. I never talked so much in my life, not even in Japanese. I'm quiet.

Grace seemed taken by the idea that it was like being in the movies. Or like fiction, I added, like a novel. She smiled and I felt really good. If I was a cat I would purr every time she smiled like that. It felt like the most perfect, most intimate and private smile. It was just for me, surely.

We did ordinary things with our time together, but ordinary things with someone extraordinary are beyond my dreams. We would go for coffee and doughnuts, for ramen, drinking *chu-hi* or *sake* or maybe wine – but I never actually liked wine. We would curl up like children under my heated *kotatsu* table. We seemed too tired and too shy to make love. It was as though we were too much in love. Can't describe it. It was enough.

Grace usually wore baggy jeans and big sweaters in grey or blue. Sometimes green, dark greens. I thought she looked like the sky and the sea and the sun. And I told her so. I would never speak like that to a Japanese girl, but I always felt confident with her. She made it easy. I would say, she made it easy to fall in love.

We walked around Shibuya and Omotesando, Harajuku, Yoyogi Park. We had no purpose, no destination. Never. And we had time, she had one more year before she would go back to her country. I was really glad. I liked her by then so, so much. I wanted her to stay. Forever. I felt something from another world, and this, this was our time. I couldn't tell anyone. I didn't want to either. I guess that made it more special. We belonged together in this other realm, this other state, and I felt that if I told anyone, anyone at all, I might break it, cause a fracture, something like that. And I didn't want to invite anyone's comments or questions. Ridicule. I wanted to enjoy what we had. I suppose I just felt so lucky, and I was afraid it might stop. Too soon. I'm selfish, but then it must have been the same for her.

As time passed, I think I stopped mentioning my future, my path. I'm not comfortable talking too much about myself, and then my upbringing and training had always been directed towards my role as a monk, and for me this time just now was to indulge in things that I might never experience again. My history studies, my fun time in Tokyo, and then, my unexpected, truly unplanned, time and love with Grace. I didn't dare hope or expect anything other, anything more. It was play. It was 'a' play. I didn't know entirely how to name it. Something beautiful for sure.

As time went on, Grace made a new friend at her university, Rei, and she was helping Grace improve her Japanese. I was pleased to hear that. She said she hadn't been sure about that level of investment before but that now that she might stay on in Japan, perhaps permanently, she should really knuckle down. I agreed with her. For me such learning had a different life and purpose. I had never been outside Japan and I imagined I would never go, and yet learning languages seemed a deeply fruitful pursuit regardless. When international visitors came to the temple in the future, I would be able to welcome them and put them at ease. Perhaps have wonderful discussions with them. And what Grace and I had, would have been so much less, so much less, had one of us not fully grasped the other's language. I didn't need English for going abroad or living abroad, I needed it to be useful to others in my own country. But Grace was ambitious, differently, and I admired this and I was truly pleased to hear that she was willing to make this effort. If she stayed in Japan, it could be a wonderful life for her, and she had better work towards fluency.

Rei began to take up quite a lot of Grace's time but I tried not to mind. Grace's free time didn't belong to me. Grace, didn't belong to me. Both of these things were true. I took a breath and then let my shoulders settle. I still felt a little irritable, but it was wrong of me and I knew I had to manage my feelings in a better way. This greediness for her was intense, but unreasonable. As I said, a more understated, lesser kind of love was fine by me. Easier to manage. And I was out of my depth to be honest, nothing to do but try to keep things in shallower waters, at least for a while. It was clear that if we were to stay together longer I'd have to become stronger, more skilled. And when that feeling, that challenge arose, it frightened me. My mind didn't need it. I had so many other challenges coming up, I had wanted this period of my life to be lighter, less demanding. I shrugged. I guess you cannot choose these things.

After a longer time than might be imagined, our shared night-times were moulded by love making, each of us bold, intense, tender, sleepy, whatever our energy was capable of. We might both weep after or laugh, just sleep, but it was a private language, and this was mostly peaceful, always ultimately, kind. And I couldn't have imagined that I would know these kinds of feelings, not at all, not at any time in my life. It made me feel vulnerable, euphoric, calmed, but it was always almost too much for me. In my ordinary existence I liked the evenness of things, a more gentle tide, and this love unsettled me. It was wonderful. And yes, it unsettled me. A lot.

Around this time, I felt that Grace became more serene, becalmed you could say. I don't mean that I wanted her to be, not some strange misogyny on my side, I wanted her to be however was good for her. And it was just my instinct that it suited her to have this greater calm. It was nice. She seemed happy, and I put much of this down to her friendship with Rei. It was clear that having a girlfriend had been a missing element for her here. Sometimes I could feel envious of what the two of them had between them. But I tried my best not to let that feeling escalate. I suppose I can only imagine Grace in very loving relationships, never anything more ordinary, never having only acquaintances, and I could never picture any other reaction to her than one of love, of closeness. I felt uncomfortable to think too much about that, but I know you never own another person.

From time to time I gave Grace small mementoes, Buddhist charms to protect her, small things from my temple back home, sometimes I gave her flowers. She always accepted them with this deep appreciation. In a way, it was uncomfortable for me, they were such small things. I'm not skilled with gifts. I didn't want her to be so grateful. But everything seemed somehow deeper and more important to her. It was hard for me to understand. I don't know why, just something lacking in me.

Grace began to talk about my country as being her true home. She would look at me for a reaction, but at least by then she accepted that reacting was not my greatest skill. Not outwardly.

For me, when I consider things overall, I think that the beginning of our relationship will always seem the most important part, all those unique moments that can never be replaced, never be compared to other moments, the simple ease in which they existed, in which they were held, the smallness. That's all. Before sex, before discussions too deep, ideas too complex, before silences that were not easily managed. Before you could ever imagine pain. I realise now, I have become a romantic man. Ha!

Rei was good for Grace, I could see it, despite the continued minor and not so minor envy that it caused me. Grace was always so delighted to have learned more about the culture and feel more immersed in our ways. It was lovely and I was happy though I didn't know quite what it meant for her or what it might come to mean. Rei introduced Grace to her family and from then on she would stay with them quite often. It became a second family for her. I was sometimes invited too but I was shy to join in. I would say that I had to study or rest but I would meet some friends, drink and smoke.

I had to be grateful to Rei for all her efforts, I knew that, all her time teaching my Grace, taking her on trips, sharing her family, but I was truly vexed at some points and had to work hard at supressing this. – This was my special time with Grace, soon I would be deep in my other studies and heading to the mountains.

At the worst point for me I punched the wall one night near my place, a concrete wall. My knuckles grazed and bled a little, the pain was mostly the rebounding of small joints after the hit. – I should talk more. – That's what I thought. Or talk less, be involved less, not have become involved at all!

I would lie about what happened to my hand. But maybe I should have been straight about it. Well, somehow everything felt the same. I explained it as frustration about my future, so it was a lie and it was also the truth and ultimately I didn't care what it was. My mind had taken up foetal position. It might be time to close down.

How many memories was Grace storing up with Rei, travels to Sado Island, to Nagoya, to Hokkaido? Grace always said that we would do more together in the future and I played along, but I didn't know what future she had in mind. She would joke about us having children, and again, though it was crazy, I played along. Somehow what we had was not fiction anymore, it was losing its poetry, it felt as though it was getting real. We were pushing it into a place it had never meant to go. We argued more and she said it was good and natural, she called our fights 'discussions'. She said it was progress and showed our maturity. I didn't agree but didn't know how to respond. My mind would get foggy and I couldn't order my thoughts all that well. I missed the sense of ease that we had shared, I missed things feeling natural. Now she had it in mind that we make 'plans'.

It came to a kind of crisis point, for me at least, when she came back from an architecture tour with Rei. They were both obsessed by Kazuyo Sejima, they had been to see some structures by her, enjoyed a talk about her work; and later they thought they'd actually caught sight of Seijima on the street and had run after her only to be mistaken. Nonetheless it had clearly been the greatest excitement.

Grace was annoyed that I didn't see how wonderful all of that had been. I explained to her that the last days I had been trying to ready myself for my training, for going away. My Buddhist training. I had to get my head around it. She took a cigarette despite not smoking. Things felt extremely uneasy. I opened a beer. I told her that I had found it difficult that she was cutting me out even before my leaving, but I was doing my best to understand. I attempted to rationalise. It made sense that she had made new friends, that she was building her own life here, and that she liked it so much, but it was hard for me to lose her before my own departure, my separate path, and that was close now.

Now Grace was the quiet one. Her cigarette burned away in the ashtray. I was clumsy, offered beer, water, tea. Nothing, she didn't want anything.

She knelt down and very quietly she began to cry. I crouched down, placed my hand on her shoulder.

But she was staying in Japan for me. She was learning the language and the culture and making friends, for me. She and Rei had half planned the wedding though they knew in truth it would be out of their hands and it would all be down to my temple. And she and I had talked of children.

I grew so nervous. Grace had always communicated so much, too much, and I communicated so little. I couldn't understand her suddenly. Too many words again and it only added to my confusion. It was as though the beauty of our fiction was being ripped away, and some ugliness of the real breezed in too boldly. Arrogantly.

This, this was my special time before I accepted my life as a monk. This was a separate, a unique, time for me. It was not part of my actual life, it was somewhere outside it. Beside it. I had been clear about this, hadn't I? Honest and sincere?

Hadn't I said that? Had I not said that we were in a movie, that it was like fiction? She gave a quiet, yes. She turned so pale and white, tears slipping away.

I tried further to explain. This time, our time together, had always been finite. This unreal, surreal, and splendid time, had been and, and would always be, the most wonderful time of my life, the best moments, memories. The greatest love.

Without knowing, I talked so much I had stopped noticing her entirely. She had swept up the deepest, most pained breath. I panicked. I took hold of her and rocked her. I didn't get it, she was like stone, but with tears, tears so heavy…

How had she not known this? I had been clear, totally clear. She wanted to remind me of talks we'd had, the future, children, the temple.

But it was all play, Grace! It was all part of our perfect play, inside this stage with all the lights shining bright. Our own precious movie. That is not life, though. That is not real life, Grace. It is not sustainable. That can only be for a time. And this, this had been our time. This had been our fiction.

Ryo

This is my *ukiyoe* museum. Welcome. You are welcome to pay me five hundred yen. Then you may enter quietly and look around the room. So many rare prints. It's dark but you understand that I have to control the light, I have to protect the colours. When I don't want you in here anymore, I will tell you to leave. I should be retired and resting, officially. So, I have the luxury of opening and closing whenever I like. I choose my own hours. And I don't need the money. Since this is the case, then why charge at all? It is to make you consider, seriously, if you wish to inconvenience me with your visit, and if your desire to view the prints is sufficient. You must deliberate this by yourself. I will not get involved. No children and no smoking. Of course, no eating and no drinking. Definitely, no dogs. Please wear a mask at all times. Don't touch anything. I don't know where you've been. And you may not use my toilet. This is my private home. It's a museum and my home.

It's true, that some people have accused me of tricking them. They say there is nothing in the museum, no prints all. Just a room with blank walls painted black. That all I aim to do is swindle, cheat visitors out of their money and use it for drink. But some people don't know well enough how to see, how to appreciate this art. It's of a higher order. If they wish to hide their ignorance and drape it in accusations, it's up to them. Let it be. John Lennon. I just do that, I let it be. They are fools, but I cannot tell them so. People shouldn't bother me. Let it be, that's all I can tell you.

Sayaka

When I was at school I fell in love. I was such a young girl, just eleven or so, and how deeply those feelings moved through me. But I suppose I did not know that's what it was, that it was love. I only knew much later on, and could only verify that that was in fact what I had felt when I had the adult mind to assess it as such. I knew though, if not in thought, then in my heart and in my veins, that it was love, and that it was romantic love. She was my teacher. My calligraphy teacher.

When my mother insisted that I had private lessons with her and at home, I resisted so hard, but she wanted me to be rounded in traditional arts and so it was decided. My mother's will was hard to fight.

Who could ever know that watching the swift and then slow movements of brush and ink could dance away with a heart so easily? I watched her hands, her wrist; observed her feline posture. I suppose I wanted to be her. No. I wanted to be near her, at least be in her orbit. And before I slept, I would have to settle myself and reassure my heart at night that I was, I *was* in her orbit, I was at least a very tiny part of her world. And she, she was a pure bright star in mine.

The years passed. I didn't have boyfriends. I didn't date. My family were bewildered. Sometimes I felt that way too. I should date! I would tell myself. Might be so nice to have a guy in my life. A boyfriend. But I never questioned it further, and I don't know why. I just never felt how many other girls must feel. I never reacted the way they did to boys and men and all that they are and all that they do. Other women seemed to react, to experience things that I never did. The lack of this, however, only ever bothered me when it bothered someone else. I was busy, always busy, with this and with that. I had kept up my calligraphy on my own, only as a hobby, but really quite a serious one. And I worked and I went hiking, and I read a lot, joined a hip-hop class, drank with friends. But there was never space for a him, a he, a man, a boy.

I liked guys. I had them as friends. I liked my father very much and my grandfather, not so much my uncle. Yes, I knew men, many men. But I did not and do not desire them.

I think I am a lesbian. Intellectually at least. Is that possible? My mind and heart steer themselves that way. I have no physical experience. I have never kissed, anyone. And I'm not sure that I will. I don't see the need to especially. For if I were to kiss someone it would have to have been her, or her very close likeness, I think. But cannot be sure.

My teacher has passed away now. I am getting old myself, I feel; so old that no one asks anymore, no one enquires, am I seeing anyone, are there any suitors, have I got my eye on anyone, a crush? But feelings don't die away with age. I will visit my mother at the weekend, she's really quite elderly now but still somewhat vital. We will collect persimmon. Yes, we will gather persimmon in the garden. And I will tell her then, when we sit and take a rest. Mother, I am a lesbian. And we will eat the fruit. And we will drink tea. I think that she will smile.

Kenji

I inherited quite a lot of money at a difficult stage. Fortunate when unfortunate. I felt I was nothing at that time. I was so grief stricken, no job, nothing. With my parents passed away I had no family. Hard to decide what to do. I sold what was familiar to me, including the house. I thought that something less familiar, far from traditional, and perhaps super new and modern, would fill me up again. I suppose that might be possible. And I wanted people. I wanted to be bonded to others, needed, relied upon, invited, included. But I didn't know how to make that happen. How to start. I didn't want to be rejected. Is that something I could buy? Even so, they might ask stuff. What is your job? Who are your family? Where do you come from?

I bought a large and modern, concrete structure. It was a former company building, a company gone bankrupt. I liked the shape of it, its immensity. I removed the heating system. That would be expensive to run. In spring I thought it was a wise move. In winter I was cold. I made a charcoal fire in a huge ceramic pot, but unless I almost sat on it, I couldn't feel a thing. Is this grief? I thought. Still now? The weather was cold, that much was clear. And is grief the same as the feeling of cold and shivering? It might just be that it is winter and I have no heating.

I went online. The place was so empty, I should fill it up. There were auctions for everything, you could ship things from anywhere, at a price. Anywhere in the entire world. I was excited. I had money, I could do whatever I wanted. It was 4am. I started to place bids. I wanted to get a table and chairs, four chairs. There were hundreds to bid on – round ones, square, and rectangular, extendable ones, extendable! I hit 'place bid' over and over and felt so alive. I'm not sure, but I think it warmed me. Someone outbid me. Who are you? How dare you? Fuck you! I hit the screen over and over. That is mine! Mine, mine, mine!

I did not sleep; I ate leftover rice and crackers. Drank a beer. Again, 'you have been outbid'. What the hell! Fuck you, fuck you whoever you are! Again and again I asserted that the table, that table, the extendable table and chairs, four chairs, were mine. Mine.

In the morning, empty cans and a bottle of strong sake lay beside me. Gross. I should tidy up. Shower.

The place was gargantuan, it was quite a walk to the bathroom for a guy with a heavy head and unsteady limbs. I ordered delivery food. – I wanted a Western bathtub, a gleaming white one. My own tiled bath was so huge it reminded me of the public baths of childhood. It made me feel lonely. Turquoise tiles. I could place a white tub in the centre, it would look like a boat at sea. I smiled to myself. I liked this idea. Later I would go online.

It was strange, I almost couldn't believe it, but yes, I could buy this thing, a white enamel bathtub, an old, authentic one just by using this auction system. One already had several bidders, another, none. Why? What's the difference? I looked as closely as I could at the images. It was hard for me. Which was better? The one seemed so popular with bidders but nevertheless, I would take a chance. I would bid on the other for safety. Back up. Suggestions popped up then, I think based on my previous bids for dining tables and chairs. Some new sets had just come online, no bidders so far. I felt a rush. Was the whole world now sleeping? Was all this choice, the chance and opportunity, just mine, all mine? I could feel my breathing, my chest heaved. I made mint tea. It helped a little. I made some bids. The things online, they looked amazing. I was hypnotised by all that design, that coolness.

I took a break and re-heated some gyosa. Chili sauce. Seriously good. Checked my bid status. Someone out there, someone, out there, was fucking things up. Get off, get off, that's mine you bastard! I hit the screen so hard, made it sticky with the chili sauce. But I just carried on. The favoured bathtub was going crazy now. It was funny but I had in my mind the various locations of these unknown bidders. I don't know why. I don't know how my brain thought it knew where they were, what country, what town. Impossible of course. But that's what I felt. I could see them, each in their own room in their own home, in Canada or the US, maybe Texas. Could be Italy, maybe Taiwan. Totally crazy. I needed to clean up the screen.

When I got back to the table after peeing, some of the auctions had ended. My heart was in my mouth. But I had won. Won and won and won! At that moment my feelings of complete and utter impotence in all areas of my life, evaporated. Gone. I felt I was a champion, and Freddie Mercury was singing that song to me. I found it online and let Freddie do his thing. I took off my shirt, popped a beer and sang with him. So loud. Ha! I won and I won and I won! No time for losers, 'cos 'I' am the champion!

The advantage of a concrete dwelling in the middle of nowhere is that you can sing with Freddie Mercury at the top of your lungs at any time of day or night! And so, I was. I was, literally, the champion… of the world. Yes!

I laughed at myself later. Broom stick for a mic stand! What the fuck! Who cares?

In the days that followed I began to think more about my life. I told myself I could be a new me. It would be exciting and fun. I might model myself on someone I admired. The guy in the coffee ads on TV, some TV talent, the other guy in the beer commercials. Any of them.

I ordered clothes rails. It was time to have a new look. From Italy I ordered shirts with fine collars; from England, brogues, handmade; from America, raincoats and again from Italy, jackets. So fine, just so, so fine!

Then things began to arrive, tables and chairs, always four chairs. Rectangular, circular, oval, square, you name it, they all began to arrive asking for space and lodging at my home. I don't know why it was, but the extendable arrived, and I didn't much like it. I would keep it always at its compact size. And then, in the days that followed, still more arrived. And more. I could not look the delivery people in the face I was so embarrassed. Often it seemed they were the same people, I knew their voices, their step, their shoes. One of them attempted to joke with me, was I opening a restaurant? I half smiled and half nodded. But no, of course I wasn't. Idiot.

Where to put all of these things? I told myself it was all alright. After all I did have sufficient space. And the large windows down the opposite side of the room permitted great views onto the black pine beyond. I could change seats often and enjoy the varied view. I could eat at a different shaped table for every meal and pretend that I was indeed dining out at a new place every night! Drinking coffee at another new place in the mornings. I had always liked that French habit of grabbing an espresso on the way to work. A kick to start the day. I had a nice coffee machine now. I had been to Paris. Once.

The black pines were diseased. Tall and thin, swaying with the weight of the wind, undermined by their sickness. Yellow ribbons decorated the worst of them, waiting to be cut down. When you are ill you will fall or be cut down. But I liked their tall thin blackness against my sky beyond. Blue, white, grey.

So, there I was with my restaurant for one.

I felt better when the shirts began to arrive and then the shoes. The shirts I hung up immediately on the rails. They were so fine and so beautiful I felt unworthy of them against my skin. – The shoes arrived in boxes of course. I tried each pair, all brogues of course, with different shaped toes, and different configurations of dots, some black, some in brown, a few in blue.

I ordered food in. Deliveries only. If anyone saw me, they would realise I don't have work, they would be suspicious of what kind of person I am. What am I doing? What's going on? No family as he only buys food enough for one. What's wrong with him? No wife, no child, no one with him. No job, no purpose, no use. And so, their eyes would tell me, the eyes of checkout staff, the eyes of other shoppers and diners, people on the street, their eyes would tell me: I am nothing. So, no. I could not go out.

The bathtubs arrived, in the end three. There was space enough for two in the bathroom and this I quite liked. I would put something in the second one. And the third I placed on the upper floor in the hallway by the long window. I might put something in that one also or else I might keep it for summer bathing! I could simply lie in it naked and through those vast windows, soak up the sun. Yes, that was the answer for tub number three. Summer bathing. Pleased, I made herb tea.

The raincoats arrived. I had not been sure of my size in the American way and so had ordered various; and as for the colour, I was not entirely certain what shade would suit me best. Of course, it needed to be black or possibly very dark blue, but in the images online in all the colours of the rainbow, I felt such a warmth. I ordered many. Very many. Then more. At first the sharp, vivid colours gripped me, then the pastel range, then the desert spectrum. All in all, burnt orange looks to be a favourite but I figured that you just never know. It's best to see it in the flesh. I took that one in short, regular and long, but of course not the extra, extra sizes. And the var-iety thrilled me. With patch pockets, side pockets, no pockets at all. Detachable hood! I settled on twenty-seven in that colour, whittled down from the sixty available options. Good. At least one of them should work well.

On the day the orange raincoats greeted me, I felt a strange euphoria. I took off all the packaging and shook each of them out and lay them over the backs of some of my dining chairs. How utterly, utterly elegant! What fine diners visited my place. Each in this most exquisite colour, notable brand, and sensible clothing – for of course, they were the most highly sought-after rainwear. I literally danced between the tables. I imagined myself some fine waiter in Paris and played out a performance serving these international guests. Among them, Freddie Mercury.

Well, I'm not sure why, but soon after I felt very weak. Per-haps too much excitement. Perhaps one too many rendition of 'I want to break free', and I realised then that I was naked, must have been some while. I touched my arm, I was quite cold.

I had made my futon up in a very tiny room. I don't know why I had chosen that one for sleeping but I had. Somehow the large rooms overwhelmed me. But in this tiny space, some might use it as a closet I suppose, small office or perhaps, most obviously a utility room, I laid my futon down and then there was really very little space left, and I guess it felt cosy. I slept and slept.

Rested, I put on my favourite raincoat and prepared myself some food. I knew how to make curry and it was quick and easy. I put rice on to cook. I found fresh socks. A large box of them.

In the days that followed I ordered more packs of curry online, beers, and a ridiculous number of snacks. I needed them to keep me going during my online work. For so it had become. My bidding, my sneak last minute snatches from the hands of others. – I moved the clothing rails into the larger rooms and then ordered more of them. One room now was filled entirely with my white Italian shirt collection. I counted them, nine-hundred and ninety-four. No, couldn't be. I checked again, and then once more. It was so. Nine-hundred and ninety-four. Disgusting, I was disgusting, I was disgusted, and this number was simply vile. I could not get online fast enough. I ordered six more. Then everything would be fine. Everything, I told myself, again, would be, fine.

The shoes stacked up so neatly. Two full rooms now. I liked to keep them in their boxes. This meant, that each time I opened the lid of one it was again a delight. I would forget the exact configurations of the dot designs, the tiny, perfect perforations. I loved them. The toe cap styles thrilled me, be it, full, wingtip, semi, quarter or longwing, though naturally full brogues, wingtips, are best. Dress shoes. Yes, dress shoes are my favourite.

Soon after, the last of the shirts arrived. I was so relieved. Just recently I had developed a fever and I was certain it was anxiety induced. I shook out the shirts and kissed the collars. I hung them up with the others and far too hot, I lay beneath them. I had opened a window and from my low position I could enjoy them, each of them pure white cotton, a thousand of them blowing in the breeze.

I'm Not David Bowie

I am not David Bowie. That's how it is. I am not. And it feels strange to be honest.

You can be me. You can be me. He said that in *Heroes*. Said it over and over, and every time I listened I believed it just a little bit more. *And you, you can be me.*

That's what I heard, what I heard him say, over and over to me and only to me during the most difficult time in my life. And I needed it. I would close my eyes and sway, and *you, you can be me* would wash over me, and dive into me. It gave me strength, you can't imagine. His words were beautiful, brilliant, and so was he. Beautiful. Brilliant. A warmth like no other. Imagine that he would share himself even with someone as hopeless as me. Simple, such a simple man, inadequate you might say, you might say wanting in every single way.

In the darkness I would sway and Bowie, your arms were wrapped around me, like lovers, and I had no idea how? How does someone be a lover? But you said to me, like lovers do, and so it was real and fantastic. And it was warm. Yes. And I thought it was this hugging kind of thing that I cannot do at all. I sometimes put a cover around my shoulders and imagined it was you.

I wanted you to hold me. I wanted to be you. And so it was. *Starman… waiting…* I shiver, then feel heat, I hear you… *in the sky…* What happens to my body? Sweat, tears. Joy! You always bring me such tremendous joy even in the fog of the most pathetic, most life depleted sorrow. I merge like a river on the tatami and need you to hold me.

Loud! And damn all my neighbours anymore! I need this! I need this! But look at me. I hesitate to turn the music up, my fingers won't allow such a move, I cannot disturb the world. I seep into the ground. I must still myself. If I died it could be better. I would like to leave no trace. No mess behind me, just rest in the soil and become part of it, harm nothing, cause no bother. Let me slip, slip, slip, slip away, as though in water.

I met Shu through a dating app. I had joined a few in the past, tentatively of course. Dating is not really for me and meeting strangers is certainly not. Huge aversion to meeting people for the first time and complete strangers are way out on the edge. But a friend gently encouraged me. Some minor contact via the app and reading some details about the women meant they were not entirely strangers. That's a lie. A well intentioned lie. Nonetheless, a lie.

And understand this, my reluctance to date was largely if not wholly related to the loss of my very first girlfriend, Ai. My only girlfriend. She was so fragile, but I failed to recognise the absolute degree of this, and her vulnerability. We are that aren't we? Fragile and vulnerable? No one so whole, so resilient that they cannot be eroded? We can just slip away, gradually or with lightening speed. And it's all too much. She starved herself, and I could not save her. Always making small plates of food and hoping that I would not overwhelm her. Persimmon, sesame tofu, eel, a little plain rice. No. And I cannot speak more.

After she passed away I wanted to understand what she had gone through, what it had felt like to grow so thin. What happened to the mind, I needed to experience it, to get close to her in the way that I had failed to do when she was alive. Then I would know what the mind sensed in that state. How she had felt and perceived things.

I had neighbours around me but I had never really got to know them. They must have known that Ai passed away but I kept my sorrow private. I was certain they never noticed me. And as my weight fell away I felt myself invisible, though inside I was quite something else.

I painted my face and stitched together fabrics to become him. I listened intently, as I had always done, as Ai had done, to Bowie, but now it was so much more intense. He was inside me, he was me. And I moved through the albums as he moved himself through me, filling me with life, lifting me with that voice. That voice. It was living in my head, it was my own voice. It was Ai and it was me.

I met up with Shu finally, Shu from the app, and we had some nice dates together in my local area. Simple dinners, beers and chatting. I told her I was David Bowie and she was amazed, so very amazed. And she could see it. That I was him. That my voice was his. I didn't mention my Ai, it would be sad, too sad. Not appropriate. Shu later came to my place, she seemed so lovely, making herself at home quite easily. Checking my things, tidying and moving things about. Much better like that, she said. I felt cared for. I would care for her too perhaps. Was it long, she asked one day, since my girlfriend died?

How did she know? And long? What is long when someone has died? Long. What does the person mean when they ask that? I don't remember answering. A moment of gaucheness on her part, a mistake. Easy to do.

She asked about Bowie. My hobby. She called it that. She wanted to know if I was aware. Of what? The neighbours, she answered. How they mocked and laughed behind my back. At the man who thinks he is David Bowie.

I told her, he had passed himself into me through his music, *and you, you can be me…* I sang it to her, and how I had felt this intense message through his eyes, and his voice deep inside me. How when Ai left, when she passed away, he wanted to protect me, and wanted to carry on through me.

The room filled with her laughter. Her destructive and immensely cruel laughter. Her stare was withering. I had mis-heard the lyrics, I had made them what I wanted them to be, I was the purest fool! 'and you, you can be mean' she roared. After all, why would Bowie choose such a pathetic soul to share his existence with, and his legacy? Why didn't I know that all the people around the town laughed at me?

I had curled up on the floor. A neighbour was at the window, she must have heard the commotion. She looked concerned. Shu didn't see her. Shu took a pan from my small kitchen and hurled it at me. I was useless and embarrassing, and still in love with a dead girl. The door slammed. I could not look again to the window. Oh, what had my sweet neighbour heard and witnessed? What kind of guest had I had in my home? What weak man was I that I just lay snivelling into the tatami?

Namiko

There was a gentle knock at my door later. I must have slept. The old lady who had been at the window now called to come inside. I apologised and picked myself up, and bid her come in. She had brought me supper and quite without looking at me, chatted away about the vegetables, all home-grown, and set the pot down in my kitchen. We all know how much you miss her, we miss Ai too, she said gently. She patted my shoulder and stepped away again and back outside.

In the morning things seemed odd. Different. The sky was bright, unusually so, and there was a humming and I realised it was from people. Tentatively, I put my head around the door. Someone called, are you dressed? Almost! I answered and I stepped back in and grabbed my t-shirt.

Outside the street was lined with all my neighbours, all the small store and restaurant owners. They looked at me, and then they sang. *And then they sang!*

And we, we can be heroes! Just for one day…

I'm not, David Bowie, of course, but I'm going to be OK now, forever and ever.

Chizuru

I followed the hand-sketched map. Looked left and right, sure this couldn't be the street. In front of me, two vast wooden gates, painted blue. I peeped between the slats, they opened onto a courtyard filled with timber. I was in Fukagawa, an area of Tokyo known historically as the timber merchants' quarter. This had to be wrong. Nevertheless, I walked in hoping to find someone to help make sense of my map, but there was no one about, just timber standing high.

I was visiting the friend of a friend from back in the UK. She'd offered to put me up while I did some research and writing in the city. In London, Junko had planned all this for me. She wanted me to meet Chizuru and have a more authentic trip. She thought it would inspire me, help me start writing poetry again, lift my spirit. I was tired though, of verse, of life. A trip had seemed a good idea. If nothing else, I thought it would do me some good to get away from people who thought you could fix everything with yoga. Sometimes a mind and a body just need rest. Real, rest. And when I told Junko how I'd like to go away awhile, to somewhere where they might respect that, she suggested her home country, and then she suggested staying with her friend who would leave me alone. Perfect. I loved Junko.

Ahead just now, under shadow, a door and a wooden stairwell. Laughter and voices suddenly from smoky throats. I looked up and to the left. Figures beyond a window, high up, in profile, seated. The outline of hands and cigarettes. I flicked my eyes to the right, a mirror image of the tree house dwelling to the left, but no light in that place, screens at the windows, no one home. I stood back and took it all in. A large timber yard; at the back and high up, something like a house, something like two houses, one to the left, one to the right, each served by a single central staircase and what looked like a narrow bridge at the very top that linked the two spaces. Everything built of wood. I heard the laughter again, men's voices – nesting birds with cigarettes. I smiled. And then startled, I turned. Thousand Cranes. Chizuru, that's what her name meant: thousand cranes. Junko had told me. And that was all that was in my head.

We stood a while, each marking the space. Attempting to maintain polite eye contact and at the same time each subtly surveying the other. Self-conscious, I wondered now what Junko might have said, how she had described me.

Chizuru laughed and read me, then told me Junko was right, I was not Marilyn Monroe. This was true, and disarming. And not being Marilyn Monroe seemed to leave a lot of space, and I began to wonder what part of that I filled and how.

Chizuru had a head of thick dark hair, just the finest wisps of grey at the margins, fifty-ish I guessed. She dressed finely in shades of aubergine and pale grey. Her scarf and skirt chosen with the eye perhaps of a craftswoman. A master of some kind. Textiles came to mind, yes, Junko had said she loved and had worked with textiles. Nothing more, I knew nothing more. What was wrong with me, why hadn't I asked about her properly? Well, there we were.

We shared warm words about knowing Junko, how I learned Japanese, how Junko was now like family. And so, our first encounter seemed to have gone quite well, and without recalling the moves in between or further conversation, I found myself halfway up the wooden stairwell following Chizuru into her home above the timber yard. It seemed eccentric. Eccentric, appealed. I felt strangely obedient in following her, and strangely comfortable with this. It felt easy. And nice.

At the top Chizuru turned to the right. To the left I heard the warm male laughter again, and cigarette smoke filtered out. Chizuru noticed and looked away. My lips parted, but it was clear I would not ask, that she would rather I did not ask, that I would earn some trust in silently accepting that this was something she would prefer not to speak of, that she might like me more if I were to stem my curiosity.

As she entered her dwelling I glanced back. The door lay open, the smoke-filled nest was covered over by a heavy beaded curtain with gaps where beads had fallen away. Two men, more? I could not tell. But two men, in vests, dirty white vests, playing cards, chain smoking. A mah-jong set close by.

Chizuru's home was vast. Inside lay room after room of tatami and sliding paper doors. The mats running in their perfect oblongs, on and on. In the centre of the dwelling was a square room with a vinyl floor. A modern oasis surrounded on all four sides by tatami rooms, and so at odds with the traditional decor. The inner room – a bruise on perfect skin.

Chizuru ushered me into the central space, and I sat at a dining table on a tall dark wood chair. I could have tea. Later I could take a bath. She would show me my room. She mentioned Junko once more and laughed again with affection. I wondered. Perhaps they had had an affair.

In the vinyl room, a synthetic island reached by paths of freshly laid tatami, I sat inert and watched as Chizuru drew back each of the paper doors and let in the light. From where I was seated, with the screens drawn back, I could see now from room to room to room, each a clever repeat of the one before. To the right and away from the tatami, the bathroom. With the door to this left ajar, I could see the bathing area quite clearly and also the tub. Clean as could be. I went to move my arm, lent on the table. And at the same time, I moved my head to try and fix on Chizuru's movements. For the moment disappeared. I glanced down. The edge of my hand and forearm had stuck to a plastic sheet that covered the table. Jam.

My eyes settled on the large thermos in the corner of the room. Junko had one in England and would fill it with boiling water in the morning, making small cups of tea throughout the day. That's what she must have meant, you could have some tea; I noticed then the stack of cups beside it, the array of tea bags individually packaged. I helped myself. Staying in the one space I scanned the place but couldn't see her. Neither could I make out her tread. Should I make her tea also? Had she gone back outside? No matter, the water would still be hot. I chose Earl Grey and moved back to the chair.

In the vinyl room almost everything was covered somehow in plastic. Either in some protective covering that it must have arrived in from the store, never removed; or like the dining table, with its transparent plastic sheet; or like the remote controls for the TV and other electrical devices, wrapped tightly in layer upon layer of cellophane. Everything, all of it, plastic. A room covered, coated, wrapped and bound in some form of prophylactic. Protecting it, keeping it safe? I pondered. Opposite were two easy chairs, electric massage chairs. Each in a thick plastic jacket, each plastic jacket coated in dust, each with an accompanying remote bound in cellophane that was sticky to the touch. I drank my tea.

The things that had arrived in plastic had been kept in plastic and other things that lacked a protective covering were given one. It looked as though it had been this way for years. Some long, long years. But beyond the vinyl floor everything was natural, tatami and shoji and walls of wood and sunlight.

I looked up. Chizuru's naked form moved distantly across the mats, her body and lithe movements belying her age. Beneath her clothes, she was perhaps just twenty. Steam rose from the right-hand side. She was taking a bath.

I looked away, and down again at my tea, refilling the cup.

The plastic room was filled with shelves, and the shelves were filled with jam. Stacked, piled up high, with jars and jars of jam. A plastic room jammed with jam. All of them imported. Every fruit you could name. Jammed with jam. I licked the side of my hand. Strawberry. And then I saw her, and I saw her notice me. I saw her notice me and pretend not to notice me, as though it was possible to retract a look. I shrank a little.

In the evening Chizuru made up a futon for me in a room made by drawing the doors to a close, making them walls. Old kimonos hung about the place, spread wide to be admired. Paper, silk and tatami. And sleeping there was easy. Perhaps the most restful sleep a person ever had.

In the morning Chizuru left early for the day, but the flask was newly filled; a rice cooker, jaws wide, placed in the centre of the table, paddle to one side; a plate of fish and vegetables close by; and a stack of Earl Grey tea bags arranged in a half moon next to a cup.

I sat and ate, and when I heard the chatter from the other side and moved to take a look, my hand again was stuck. Apricot.

Patterns emerged in our brief dance around each other. Chizuru would rise before me and eat her bread and jam breakfast and a handful of colourful pickles; laying out a Japanese breakfast for her house guest. She would be gone for the day and I would clean up after us and bathe away the jam.

She instructed me not to speak with the men in the dwelling opposite. She had not spoken with them in years and did not care to. But when I returned to the timber yard at lunchtime one day, I met with the duo on the bridge between the dwellings. Politely we exchanged greetings, and I re-entered Chizuru's home to settle back to writing there.

A short while later, a small and smoky voice called out, and when I went to answer, the men in vests held dishes of food, and thought I might have need of lunch. They liked to break after their morning's work, though their sister would describe them as lazy. In the afternoons they played mah-jong. I could join them if I liked. But in any case, they hoped the clicking of the mah-jong tiles did not disturb me. I told them it did not, that in fact, I liked it. They nodded and smiled and I joined them for lunch. They asked only that I did not tell their sister of their visit. Chizuru, of course.

And so, the second secret pattern emerged. Each day I would take lunch with the mah-jong brothers and sometimes share a beer; and in the afternoons I would research and write, the gentle clatter of tiles and laughter in the distance.

Years later I would miss the jam and vinyl; the trails of smoke-filled laughter from across the bridge. Chizuru-san and her mah-jong brothers. And I was always left to wonder just why they never spoke.

I bought pickles and beer forever afterwards. And sometimes, jam.

(An earlier incarnation of this story was published in *New Welsh Review* literary magazine in 2013. It was titled: Tokyo Spaces)

The Miniatures

Yume

The tree was bare. Its bark turned white – was it sick?
The sky was white. And the ground?
Just stones. White, white stones.
White tree, white earth, sky white.

And in the morning, there was snow. White, white, snow.
        Oh, tree!
Brush away the snow. Away, away, away.
And the tree is bare.
The sky is white. And stones. All white.
Should have apples. Trees, should.
No leaves, no apples.
White stones at the base.
And was the tree dead? And it looked so lonely.

Apple. Bring the tree an apple.
Bright red apple. Place at the base of the trunk.
White, white. Red apple. Blue.

Setsuko

Woman, I am
I speak one language.
I know myself.
I speak another language.
I know myself, new.

I live in my country.
I know it. And I know myself.
I live in another country.
It is new. And I am new too.

I live in my head.
And I know myself.
I am quiet. I am speaking. I am sleeping.
All by myself.

I live in my heart.
And I know myself.
I am strong. I'm weak. I'm just OK.
I am myself. I am my SELF.
And it is wonderful.

Maru-chan

I like to draw. Dots. Only dots. Lots of dots.

Kanayo – Sakka

My ambition for the next life is not to be a writer, but to be the cat that sleeps upon the writer's desk.

Joso

There is nothing in this world you need to know that cannot be learned from a cat.

Namiko

Acknowledgements

I am ever grateful to my editor, Mick Felton for believing in the work I do, and to everyone at my publisher, Seren, for all their hard work, patience and creative energy in bringing the book into the world and getting it noticed. So, thank you so much Simon, Sarah and Jamie to name but a few, you are much appreciated.

Special thanks to Arts Council England for the continued support for my writing, it has been invaluable.

My very deep thanks also, to the Daiwa Anglo-Japanese Foundation, for their travel and research grant which enabled me to plunge my hands into Japanese soil again and hopefully enrich the stories I continue to tell about contemporary Japan.

And Namiko, your MANGA is always a delight, and I am so very honoured that you agreed to illustrate the book. Ever grateful, Jayne

My Falling Down House

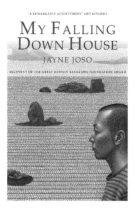

I had come here because I was drawn to the place; there was a feel for nature here, a sense of a slow and simple way of living. A forgotten way of living.

A wood and paper house, a man, a cat and a cello. This is the Tokyo of former 'salaryman' Takeo Tanaka after the financial crisis, after the tsunami.

"An unacknowledged gem: subtle, allusive, and deceptively ambitious." – *New York Times*

"*My Falling Down House* is a masterpiece." – *Anne Janowitz*

"Set in contemporary Japan … it speaks simultaneously to contemporary globalizing society. A remarkable achievement." – *Sho Konishi*

"This is a novel for anyone who has had a setback in life; for anyone who ever thought of escaping reality and retreating into the shadowy imagination. A beautiful exploration of identity by a hugely talented writer." – *Eluned Gramich*

From Seven to the Sea

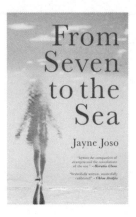

Esther must negotiate adult dysfunction, and a school environment that exposes her to prejudice and injustice. *From Seven to the Sea* is a window on to the world of a seven-year-old who rejects convention and expectation. Instead, Esther embarks on a creative expedition into liberty and freethinking; every day, in place of school, she sets out to sea.

"With this tender story of trauma in a child's life, brimming with sympathy and insight, Jayne Joso hymns the compassion of strangers and the consolations of the sea." – Horatio Clare

"A beautifully written and masterfully calibrated portrayal of the search for sanctuary and enchantment within a childhood under siege." – *Chloe Aridjis*

"A charming story, held together by the well-wrought character of Esther and Joso's remarkable talent for rendering her inner life believably. Esther's optimism and lack of guile remind the adults reading it of the wisdom of children."
– *The Cardiff Review*